The Price of
Paradise

Collect all the exciting new Doctor Who *adventures:*

DOCTOR·WHO

The
Price
of
Paradise

BY COLIN BRAKE

BOOKS

Published by BBC Books, BBC Worldwide Ltd,
Woodlands, 80 Wood Lane, London W12 0TT

First published 2006
Reprinted 2006 (twice)

ISBN-13: 978 0 563 48652 7
ISBN-10: 0 563 48652 X

Commissioning Editor: Stuart Cooper
Creative Director and Editor: Justin Richards
Production Controller: Peter Hunt

Doctor Who is a BBC Wales production for BBC ONE
Executive Producers: Russell T Davies and Julie Gardner
Producer: Phil Collinson

Cover design by Henry Steadman © BBC 2006
Typeset in Albertina by Rocket Editorial Ltd, Aylesbury, Bucks
Printed and bound in Germany by GGP Media GmbH

For more information about this and other BBC books,
please visit our website at www.bbcshop.com

For Kassia and Cefn

It was another perfect day in paradise. Sister Serenta could feel the warm golden sand between her toes as she walked barefoot along the beach, her moccasins in her hand. Saxik, the Fire Lord, was high in the sky, making the waves shimmer as they rolled gently on to the shore, sending bubbling sheets of sparkling water dancing over her feet. A gentle breeze cooled her brow, tempering the heat.

Half a dozen cream-coloured sea birds were whirling in the sky. Serenta thought they looked as if they were playing some kind of game, chasing each other, zooming high and low and then floating without effort on the hot thermal currents. Sometimes, when she had been younger, Serenta had wondered how it would feel to fly like a bird, but now she was almost an adult she knew how silly that idea was.

She glanced down at the wicker basket she was

carrying. A few juicy red glasnoberries rolled around at the bottom, but only a handful. She knew she should have had a full basket by now. Laylora provides, she thought to herself with a smile, but we still have to do our bit.

She started back into the forest to find the others. Her brother, Purin, and his friend Aerack were digging a new killing pit – the animal traps the Tribe of the Three Valleys used to catch wild pigs. Serenta was meant to be helping them by weaving a cover for the pit from vines and leaves, but she'd got bored and had decided to go and find them something to eat instead.

As she walked back through the trees she could feel herself tensing up. The forest was quite dense here and the thick canopy of leaves cast deep shadows. Despite the afternoon heat she started to shiver. Something was wrong, she could feel it in her bones; a tangible air of dread. For the first time in her life, Serenta found herself frightened by the forest that she knew so well.

As she approached the place where the boys had been working it seemed to get even darker. She could hear something moving ahead of her, but it wasn't the sound of digging or voices. If anything it sounded like an animal. Was it a boar? Had one stumbled into the killing pit before it was finished? And, if it had, were Purin and Aerack all right?

Serenta called their names nervously as she got nearer, unable to hide the alarm in her voice. There was no answer. She stopped in her tracks. Something was moving towards her, something large, and it wasn't her brother or Aerack; it was something much more frightening. Serenta turned and ran, scarcely able to believe her eyes.

It couldn't be. It was impossible. She must have imagined it. But there was no doubting the crashing sounds made by the thing that was now chasing her through the trees. She glanced back over her shoulder and got another fleeting impression of the creature behind her. This was no wild boar; it was a biped like herself, but much larger, hairy and bestial-looking. Vicious sharp talons at the end of each arm were slicing through the forest like machetes, cutting a direct path through the trees and bushes.

She ran on blindly, fear driving her forward. Her heart felt as if it would burst through her chest at any moment. The undergrowth was ripping at her legs, leaving a mess of bloody scratches, but she didn't let this slow her down. She was nearly back at the beach now, but there was no let-up in the sounds of pursuit.

As her feet began to run on sand rather than earth, she risked another look over her shoulder and paid a terrible price – her foot caught on a piece of driftwood and suddenly she was flying through the air. She landed heavily on the beach in a cloud of soft sand. Coughing, she rolled over on to her back and found herself in the shadow of the beast. Staring up at it, she realised that she had been right.

All her life Serenta had heard stories of the mythical

monsters that were said to appear when her planet was in danger, but she'd always thought they were just tales to scare children. Yet now one of these legendary protectors of Laylora was right here – looming over her and blocking out Saxik's light. Her last thought, as the beast knocked her unconscious, was that nothing would ever be the same again.

The Witiku had risen!

ONE

'Mercury in the side pocket,' announced the Doctor with confidence.

Rose just laughed. 'You can't – you can't get near Mercury without going through Jupiter.'

The Doctor grinned and wiggled his eyebrows at her before approaching the snooker table to take his shot. Holding the cue behind his back – in his best showman style – he took careful aim. Thwack! The cue slid forward and kissed the cue ball, which shot off in the opposite direction, flying away from the ball the Doctor had called.

As Rose watched, open-mouthed, the white ball bounced off one cushion, then another, before heading directly towards the brown 'Mercury' ball. It completely missed the yellow ball that represented Jupiter. After a display like that, Rose wasn't surprised when the Mercury ball responded by rolling, ever so gently, into the side pocket that the Doctor had nominated.

'Right – just the Earth, then, and you'll have to concede,' said the Doctor, smiling, and took aim again.

The blue-green ball representing Earth was actually a perfect model of the planet. Rose had held it up to the light and seen all the landmasses marked in miniature.

'If I just hit it round about California…' The Doctor leaned over the table and lined up his shot. Click! The Earth ball went spinning into the pocket. 'Game over! I thought you were meant to be good at this?'

'I am,' retorted Rose, annoyed. 'But where I come from we play snooker with reds and colours, not planets.'

The Doctor grinned his most enthusiastic grin and Rose found it difficult to be cross about losing. They were waiting for the TARDIS navigational systems to reset themselves after a wild and exciting comet chase and, to pass the time, the Doctor had produced this fold-out snooker set from somewhere.

'Picked this up in the far future,' he had explained, as he placed the small-suitcase-sized box on the floor in the console room. 'Retro-gaming was really big in the fifty-eighth century.' And Rose had watched, amazed, as the Doctor had opened the case, which, impossibly, unfolded itself to become the entire snooker table, the balls and the cues.

'How does it all fit in that little box?' she had asked.

The Doctor had just winked at her. 'Hard light compression,' was his baffling reply.

'You what?'

'You really don't want to know.'

Rose moved to reset the planets on the table. 'Best of three?'

The Doctor shook his head. 'That's enough rest and relaxation, I reckon.' He flicked a switch on the table and the entire thing folded back in on itself, returning to its suitcase form.

'Why? Are we there yet?' Rose was deliberately whining, like a back-seat child, while grinning at the same time.

'The TARDIS should have had time to recalibrate by now,' the Doctor answered in all seriousness. 'So with a bit of luck we'll be landing soon.'

With a sudden burst of energy he was already at the central control console, checking the various readouts and fiddling with switches and levers.

'Where are we going, then?' Rose asked.

'I don't know actually,' the Doctor confessed. 'I hooked up your MP3 player to the TARDIS controls and hit Shuffle. We're either going to find ourselves at a totally random destination...'

'Or?'

'Or we end up inside Franz Ferdinand!' The Doctor grinned to show he was joking. 'Let's find out...' And he yanked one of the large levers down, sending the TARDIS towards its next port of call.

It had been a long night for the Tribe of the Three Valleys, and it looked set to be a long morning too. For hours after the three youths had failed to appear for the evening meal search parties had scoured the forest, looking for them, but eventually it had become too dark and the search had had to be abandoned.

Mother Jaelette washed her face in the stream at the edge of the village and wondered what more they could do. In the hours since dawn they had searched again, but there was still no sign of Aereck, Purin or Serenta. Brother Hugan had taken off for the ancient temple to ask the benevolent living planet to return their lost children, but Jaelette preferred to put her hope in more practical means. Right now it was important that life went on as usual. Panicking was not going to help. Wherever the three teenagers had got to, there had to be a rational explanation for their disappearance. Perhaps something had surprised them at the killing pit and they had escaped into the inland mountains to hide? Jaelette shook her head, causing her pitch-black ponytail to whip her neck. None of the possibilities she thought of seemed to make very much sense.

As she walked back among the tents that made up the village she could see the various members of the tribe going about their morning routines and, for a moment, it almost felt as if the whole thing had been a terrible nightmare. Then Jaelette caught sight of her younger sister, Healis, the mother of two of the missing children, trying not to cry. Jaelette hurried over and put a reassuring arm around her sister, muttering some words of encouragement. Healis buried her head in her sister's chest and sobbed.

With most of the men away, moving the animals to the winter grazing lands, and most of the elders too ancient to make much sense of anything, Mother Jaelette was effectively the leader of the village. She knew the others would look to her for wisdom, but this time she had no idea what to tell them. All she could hope was that somehow Brother Hugan's ritual would have the desired effect. Jaelette had precious little time for the witch doctor and his fascination with the old ways, but right now she would be happy to settle for some divine intervention.

In the darkness of deep space, in an absolute vacuum, very little ever happens. In this particular part of space, nothing much had moved for thousands of years. Until now. Without any warning, space and time burped, warped and wibbled, and, where a moment ago there had been nothing, a spaceship appeared.

It wasn't the most exciting-looking deep-space craft that had ever left a space dock. Its once-gleaming silver panels were now grimy with space dust and pocked with more dents than a teenager's face. Over the years makeshift repairs had changed the original sleek lines of the craft until not even its own designer would have recognised it now. The hyperspace engines, salvaged from a wrecked freighter, were bolted on with no regard for aesthetics and an entire section of the hull near the rear had been recycled from a disused navigational beacon.

The SS *Humphrey Bogart* had started life as a rich man's toy – a sleek speedster for nipping around the owner's home system between the numerous houses he had on different planets. Unfortunately, as is often the case, the man's fortune had not been entirely the result of honest endeavour, and when the authorities finally caught up with him, the spaceship had been one of the first of his assets to be repossessed. The tax authorities had used it for a while, but then it had been commandeered and pressed into military service in a nasty and protracted space war. Finally, many years later and almost a wreck, it had come into the possession of its present owner. Professor Petra Shulough, the academic and explorer, had decided that it would be the perfect vehicle for her explorations. In truth, the only perfect thing about it was the price.

Designed originally for a crew of thirty, the manuals claimed that it could fly with a bare minimum manning level of twelve. The professor wasn't keen on technicalities like safe manning levels. Her crew numbered just four: her captain, Major Kendle, and three youngsters – two fresh out of the Space Naval Academy and one bored rich kid with a history of space-yacht racing and an adrenalin addiction.

In space, as the old saying has it, no one can hear you

yawn, thought Trainee Pilot Jonn Hespell as he sat watching the read-outs on his screen cycle through yet another automated sequence. Once again the ship's AI ran the standard scans, testing the results against the incomplete data Professor Shulough had provided.

Hespell, a thin, nervous-looking young man with spiky red hair, glanced over at the academic who had recruited him and the rest of the crew, and set them on this apparently endless mission. Shulough must have been the same age as his mother, but with her short white hair and lined face she looked older. Her sharp features were always fixed in an expression without any hint of softness. In the eighteen months he had served on the *Humphrey Bogart*, Hespell didn't think he had ever seen her smile.

A flashing green light from his screen caught his eye – something new at last! He took in the information and immediately ran a manual check on the data. To his surprise, it tallied. The scans had made a match. Surely this would bring a smile to the professor's face? He spun around in his seat and cleared his throat to attract her attention.

'Professor?' he began, but he got no further as she was already up and out of her seat.

'You have something?' she demanded, but he didn't need to answer as she had already started to take in the information on his display.

If Hespell had really expected a smile he was to be disappointed. There was barely a shift in the tone of her voice; perhaps just the slightest hint of excitement.

'Plot a new course, Mr Hespell. If this scan is right…
we're about to finally reach the Paradise Planet!'

Hespell made the adjustments and, with only a little
grumbling and complaining, the spaceship's engines
responded. The *Humphrey Bogart* moved forward
through the inky depths of space.

Brother Rez and Sister Kaylen knelt quietly in front of
the Table of Gifts. The big stone altar was the
centrepiece of the huge main chamber of the ancient
temple. In front of them the shaman himself was
walking back and forth, muttering a ritual chant and
scattering jinnen powder on the floor. Kaylen glanced
sideways at Rez, catching his eye. She had to bite her
lip to stop herself from bursting out laughing, despite
the seriousness of the situation. Rez narrowed his
eyes, urging her to get a grip.

Kaylen looked at him and smiled. How he had
changed since she had found him all those years ago!
She had been only a child herself, but she could
remember the day they met as clearly as if it were
yesterday.

It had been the sound that she heard first. A sharp
cracking retort like a massive tree being split by a giant's
axe, then a rumble like her father's snoring but much,
much louder. Kaylen, just six years old and bright as a
button, had been on the beach. She was meant to be
collecting firewood but was picking up shells instead.

Kaylen remembered hearing a pair of mylan birds calling to each other. Even as a small child, that melodic trilling had always made her heart sing in harmony. She had decided to spend just five more minutes on the sand, even though she knew it meant Mother Jaelette would be cross with her again.

'Everyone has to do their bit,' Mother Jaelette used to tell her every morning. 'The tribe is your family and everyone has their part to play.' Which meant doing chores: finding firewood, or harvesting the jinnen crop, or sweeping out the tents. Kaylen never really understood why it all involved such hard work. Laylora provided for them, didn't she? Why did anyone have to do chores? Just ten more minutes, she said to herself, revising her previous promise. And she got comfortable on the warm sand and closed her eyes.

That's when she heard the sound, ripping the peace of the late afternoon into shreds. At first she couldn't work out where it was coming from. She sat up, startled. What was it? Was Laylora angry with her for not doing her chores? The noise grew even louder and it seemed to be coming from above. Shielding her eyes from the full glare of Saxik with her arm, Kaylen looked up and was shocked to see a plume of black smoke stretching across the sky, as if someone had scratched a dirty line through the heavens. Something was falling. She followed the smoke with her eyes and saw a dark object at the front of the plume. As she watched, it plummeted into the forest with a final scream of sound and suddenly there was silence.

Bravely – or stupidly – Kaylen decided to investigate rather than get help. As she got closer to the point of impact she found a scene of total devastation. Something had torn through the forest, uprooting trees and scorching vegetation, leaving an ugly scar. Eventually it had torn a groove into the ground itself, a deepening channel that was still smoking as Kaylen gingerly followed it. Finally she reached the object itself.

It was smaller than she'd expected, not much bigger than her father: a metal egg, blackened and burnt after the rapid descent. Kaylen had never seen anything like it before in all her six years. Despite her fears, she crept closer. She was trying to remember the stories that Brother Hugan was always telling the children, about the old days when Laylora's guardians would stalk the land. Was it possible that the Witiku were born from metal eggs like the one in front of her? Brother Hugan said that the Witiku would return if they were needed. But the Witiku only attacked to protect Laylora, didn't they? Kaylen was sure she had done nothing to upset her planet. Her mother maybe, but not the planet!

Hardly daring to breathe, Kaylen reached the object. It was steaming hot; the air above it rippled in an intense heat haze. Suddenly there was a hiss of escaping air and a hatch began to open. Kaylen jumped back, alarmed and scared, and for a moment she considered running away. But something stopped her in her tracks. It was a sound from inside the metal egg, a sort of gurgling.

Forcing herself to turn back, Kaylen walked right up to the hatch, which had now opened fully, and looked inside. She could see some sort of bed, and strapped securely into it was the thing that was responsible for making the strange new noise. Kaylen could hardly believe her eyes. A moment ago she had been scared to within an inch of her life, but now she felt all that fear melting away and she began to laugh with surprise and delight. The creature inside the egg began to laugh as well, chuckling with pleasure in response to Kaylen's smiling face. This was no monster from myth and legend; this was a tiny, vulnerable creature that needed her. Small and helpless, with chubby little arms and chubby little legs, it was a baby!

That had been fifteen years ago. Now that baby was glaring at her and asking her to take the shaman's ritual seriously. Kaylen smiled at the thought of it. Rez had grown into a handsome young man, fit and tanned, and taller than most of the Laylorans he lived among. Kaylen had grown up too; she was now an attractive young woman with a fierce intelligence and a wicked sense of humour. Despite the six-year age gap between them, the Layloran and her stepbrother were very close. It was because of Rez that Kaylen found herself here today, in the ancient temple, trying not to laugh at the shaman.

It seemed to Kaylen that the years had not been kind to poor Brother Hugan. When she was a child, she had been terrified of the shaman and everything he stood for, but now all that had changed. He cut a rather sad and pathetic figure, dressed up in his bright robes and his mylan-feather headdress. His face was painted with streaks of colour that were meant to make him look fierce, but to her he simply looked silly. Underneath the carnival costume and the make-up, Brother Hugan was just another old Layloran, one in the twilight years of his life, who had a sad obsession with the way things used to be.

Although the modern Laylorans inhabited a tented village, living off the land in harmony with the seasons, their more primitive ancestors had enjoyed a different relationship with the world. The ancients had worshipped Laylora as a goddess and their religious rites had included blood sacrifice. Brother Hugan spent hours in the ancient temple, studying the old ways, seeking opportunities to revive some of the less objectionable aspects of their practices in accordance with tribal history. It was an uphill battle with the younger generation, though. Kaylen and her contemporaries, although still respectful of the natural order of things, were less inclined to see the planet as a living deity.

Ironically it was Rez, the outsider, who had most time for Brother Hugan and his stories of the old ways.

Perhaps it was because, as he grew older, he became more aware of the things that set him apart from the others – the differences between his physical form and that of the Laylorans – and sought a way to integrate himself more closely with the tribe. So when other young Laylorans poked fun at the shaman and ignored his stories, Brother Rez took it all in.

And where Brother Rez went, Sister Kaylen went too. When her niece, nephew and Aerack disappeared, Brother Hugan had announced that they would need to make an offering to Laylora at the ancient temple. Rez had immediately volunteered himself and, of course, his stepsister to assist in the ritual.

Kaylen looked up and realised with a start that the shaman was walking towards her. She tried to arrange her features into a suitably serious expression but found it a struggle.

'Sister Kaylen, will you assist me with the jinnera?'

Kaylen nodded and crossed to the fire that was burning in a grate in the corner of the room. A kettle of liquid was bubbling away, suspended from a frame. Kaylen carefully removed the kettle and poured the thick brown liquid into three ancient carved wooden cups. The three of them took a cup each and approached the sacred altar, behind which a statue of a woman – an incarnation of Laylora – stood.

The jinnera, a drink made using the jinnen beans that grew so abundantly in the jungle, had a sharp, slightly bitter taste that was unpleasant at first but quickly became addictive. Kaylen could smell the exotic aroma wafting up from the cup and hoped the bit in the ceremony where they drank it on behalf of Laylora was coming soon. But Brother Hugan seemed to have other ideas. He stepped forward to the altar and placed his cup down between himself and the statue. He nodded at Rez and at Kaylen to do the same. A moment after they had placed their own cups on the altar, the shaman raised his arms high in the air and threw his head back.

'O mighty Laylora, the provider of all, we your humble servants ask for your kindness…'

Kaylen closed her eyes – this sounded as if it might go on for a long time. And it did. It seemed that Brother Hugan wanted to name-check every fruit, nut and leaf that the generous Laylora had provided for her chosen people. Kaylen opened her eyes to see what was going on and found herself looking down into her cup at the jinnera she desperately wanted to drink. But there was something wrong. The surface of the liquid was vibrating. No – not just the liquid; the cup itself was shaking and moving!

'Brother Hugan…' she began, but her companions were already aware that something odd was happening.

The very ground itself was rumbling. Suddenly Kaylen found herself staggering as the earth beneath her feet moved, spilling her precious drink. Now the whole temple was shaking and parts of the ancient walls were breaking free and falling all around them. She remembered the stories she had been told as a child, of how Laylora had shaken them out of living in buildings like these to pursue a more nomadic lifestyle.

'What is it?' Rez asked his stepsister, as he tried to pull her a safe distance from the walls, but it was the shaman who answered him.

'It's Laylora – she's angry with us!' he ventured.

At that moment it was easy to believe. Everything was wrong. The temple that had seemed so solid and permanent was shaking like one of their tents in a winter storm. Laylora was a world of peace and limitless bounty – why was it turning on them like this? Kaylen could see that Rez was as scared as she was, but Brother Hugan was just angry. And then, as suddenly as it had started, it was all over. The ground beneath their feet felt solid again.

'I don't understand,' she complained. 'Why is Laylora angry?'

Brother Hugan shook his head. 'It's another sign. Like everything else. That's why those three youngsters have disappeared. Laylora is angry and we will all perish in her wrath!'

He turned on his heels and stalked off, leaving the ritual unfinished and the spilt jinnera offering pooling on the ground.

The mood on the bridge of the spaceship was tense, to

say the least. The *Humphrey Bogart* was entering the outer reaches of a solar system but it was not a straightforward approach. In fact it was a veritable minefield. A massive cloud of meteorites and planetary debris made an almost impenetrable barrier protecting the five planets closest to the system's class-three star. As soon as it became clear that some very fine piloting would be required if the ship was to pass through this belt unscathed, young Hespell had relinquished the helm to the captain. Major Kendle was Professor Shulough's right-hand man. Like the ship, the major had seen action in wartime and bore the physical and mental scars to prove it. He was in his late sixties now, still fit but long since retired from military service.

Hespell looked on in awe as the veteran space marine steered the ship manually, his eyes fixed on the screen. He knew the older man had been trained to stay cool under fire but this was something else. With a light touch on the navigational controls and hardly looking at the instruments at all, he was displaying the sort of old-fashioned, seat-of-your-pants flying that the academy just couldn't teach. Kendle had nerves of steel and the reflexes of a panther – a winning combination. Nevertheless, Hespell found he had to remind himself to breathe as he watched their slow forward progress.

He looked around the bridge and saw that the rest of the crew were reacting in the same way. At the communications console even Jae Collins, whose perpetual air of boredom always rankled with Hespell, seemed tense. Jae looked about eighteen but was a few years older than that, which made him about the same age as Hespell. However, the two men could not have been more different. Hespell worked hard and obeyed the rules; Jae – born to a family of intergalactic lawyers – had never had to work for a credit in his life and believed rules were merely there to be broken. Hespell couldn't quite work out why Jae had volunteered for this mission. Perhaps he had expected it to be more exciting. Well, it was certainly getting exciting now.

The final member of the crew sat beside Hespell at the navigational and ship management consoles. Hespell let his gaze linger on Ania Baker for a second and then had to look away quickly, turning red, when she shot a little sideways glance at him. The pretty, petite brunette with the round, open face looked as fragile as a porcelain doll, but he knew she was a tough cookie underneath. Ania had been a cadet with him at the academy, but he had never managed to speak to her in his five years there. On board the *Humphrey Bogart* they had finally become friends. Beneath her calm exterior, he was pretty sure, she would be feeling the same tension they all were.

All of them with one exception, that is. At the back of the crew, Professor Shulough was leaning against the wall, sipping from a mug of coffee, looking utterly relaxed. It was amazing. Hespell wasn't sure exactly how long the professor had been searching for this mysterious planet, but he knew it was a matter of years not months. How could she be so cool now that they were on the verge of finding the holy grail she had been searching for all this time? Looking at the professor calmly finishing her drink, the young pilot wondered if she was quite human.

'Professor, we're through!'

Kendle's speech was a low growl at the best of times, but even Hespell could hear the relief in his voice. On the main screen the third planet of the star system could now be seen in all its glory. And it was glorious – a beautiful green-blue gem of a planet. Was this really the fabled Paradise Planet?

Without warning the ship suddenly shook violently. The horizontal became vertical as the ship's internal gravity generator went off-line. Every console and every instrument fell dark. Screams filled the air as the crew members, none of whom were strapped into their seats, were thrown around the room. Then the spacecraft began to spin.

'Are we under attack?'

It was the professor from somewhere over his shoulder. Hespell hoped she'd managed to grab hold of something when whatever it was had hit them.

'Some kind of EMP,' came the calming tones of Kendle.

An electromagnetic pulse? Hespell was amazed – it would have had to be enormously powerful to break through their shields and cause such a total shutdown.

'Electrical power is out. The emergency generators are coming on-line but we can't reboot all the systems at the same time.'

'Life support?'

'Priority number one. Then defence shields and engines. But we're caught up in the gravity well of the planet. I can't maintain this orbit.'

'We'll have to try and land, then…'

'It might be a bumpy ride… Hold on…'

The next few moments were among the most frightening and yet exhilarating that Hespell had ever experienced. In the emergency red lighting that flooded the bridge, the crew responded professionally to the crisis, setting in motion the routines they had practised in every training drill. Each of them had specific crash-landing duties. Even cool Jae Collins seemed scared for once, as he too responded to the emergency. And in the middle of all the activity, there was Major Kendle wrestling with the steering controls, trying to ensure that their descent into the planet's atmosphere was at a safe angle. A few degrees out and the ship would burn up before it even had a chance to crash.

While the major struggled to save their lives, Hespell set about his own emergency task, which was to launch a distress beacon. If the crash-landing went badly, this might be their only hope of rescue. Battery-powered, it would send out a looped SOS signal into deep space. As Hespell launched the beacon, he couldn't help crossing his fingers for luck. He knew they would need it; their search for the Paradise Planet had taken them far from the busy space lanes and more populated areas of space. Was anybody likely to hear their cry for help?

Leaving Rez at the temple to help clear up after the earth tremor once Brother Hugan had abandoned them, Kaylen hurried back through the forest alone. She wanted to make sure everyone in the village had survived. Having seen the devastation at the temple, she was worried that the tents would have been utterly destroyed.

In her haste, she was running without really looking where she was putting her feet. Twigs and vines slapped her legs and face as she hurtled through the forest, but she didn't let that slow her down. Although she didn't believe in Brother Hugan's talk of disaster, she couldn't help wondering if perhaps the old man was right after all. Perhaps something bad was coming.

Suddenly her foot caught on a root and she found herself flying forward. Kaylen hit the ground awkwardly and winded herself. As she lay on her back for a second, trying to catch her breath, she heard a noise that she had heard just once before. A resounding boom echoed around the sky, sending thousands of birds squawking into the air in panicky flight. She looked up and was not disappointed. It was happening again… just like before. Ugly black smoke was scrawled across the sky. Something was coming. Something alien.

TWO

Rose watched as the Doctor hurried from panel to panel of the TARDIS console, tweaking settings, flicking switches and tapping the odd read-out. This was one of her favourite parts of time and space travel: the last minutes inside the ship before stepping out into… who knew what. The past, the future, sideways into another universe – every time Rose opened those doors she could be certain that the TARDIS had landed somewhere new, exciting and different. Even the time it had taken them to Clacton. In the winter. Even that had been fun – once they had managed to persuade the Italian ice cream man to open up his shop and they'd been able to walk along the beach eating 99s in the persistent drizzle.

Rose wondered idly what might be outside this time when she walked out of the police box doors. Disturbing her reverie, without warning, the TARDIS shuddered and jerked violently, sending her flying. The console room was filled with an urgent screeching alarm Rose couldn't remember hearing before.

'What is it?' she asked, getting to her feet gingerly, once the worst of the lurching seemed to be over.

'Alarm of some kind,' came the answer, as the Doctor's hands moved with amazing speed over the controls, trying to locate the source.

'I sorta knew that,' said Rose, 'but what kind? Red alert? Mauve? Orange? Is something up with the TARDIS?'

The Doctor shook his head. 'No, it's not one of ours.' A quick grin. 'Not this time!' He slammed down a lever and the noise abruptly ceased.

'It's gone!' Rose observed, but the Doctor was still dancing around the multi-sided control console, deep in concentration.

'I just turned the volume down. Can't hear yourself think with that going on, can you?'

The Doctor was now looking at the computer screen, on which pages of data were streaming by at an astonishing rate. Rose moved closer but things were, as usual, meaningless to her. Although the TARDIS could translate any spoken or written language for her, it never seemed to want to help her read the Doctor's peculiar script of curves and circles.

'It's an intergalactic mayday... A star ship is in trouble.'

'Can we help?' Rose was sure the Doctor would be able to do something. Like an intergalactic AA man.

The thought of the Doctor dressed in a bright yellow jacket made her smile.

'I'm reconnecting the directional controls.' Again the Doctor's hands flashed over the console. 'I promised you a magical mystery tour this time... and you're going to get one.'

The TARDIS engines shifted into a new gear – a sound Rose knew meant that they were about to arrive somewhere.

On the planet's surface, in the area of Laylora inhabited by the Tribe of the Three Valleys, a sudden wind whipped up from nowhere. The few birds that had returned to the tree tops, having been frightened away by the sonic boom of the crashing spaceship, were now spooked for a second time. Accompanied by a tremendous rasping sound, a blue box appeared, faint at first, but rapidly becoming solid. With a final thump, the TARDIS finished its arrival. A moment later the doors opened and Rose appeared, wide-eyed and intrigued to discover where they had landed now.

'Wow!' she gasped, and took a couple of steps forward.

The ground was mossy and springy under her feet and the air was slightly sweet. To one side of her, Rose could see a rich green forest disappearing into the distance, where she could faintly make out glorious snow-tipped mountains. In the other direction was an image from every Caribbean holiday brochure that she had ever seen: a perfect desert-island beachfront, consisting of endless white sands and a beautifully inviting turquoise sea. She turned back to shout into the TARDIS interior.

'I think I need my bikini and a beach ball!'

But the Doctor was already stepping through the doors, shrugging into his long brown coat. He quickly locked the doors behind him, preventing any chance of a change of clothes. 'Hello? Emergency distress call… Crashed spaceship… Any of this sound familiar?' he reminded her.

Rose instantly felt guilty. She had been so taken with the stunning surroundings that she'd totally forgotten what had brought them here.

'Are you sure this is the right place?' she asked, hiding her embarrassment with a hint of belligerence. She waved an airy hand around her at the general beauty. 'I mean, I don't know about you, but I'm seeing holiday paradise, not a disaster site.'

The Doctor put his arms on her shoulders and gently turned her around. 'How about that?'

He pointed behind the TARDIS, where, in the far distance, an ugly column of thick black smoke rose from the forest floor.

'OK, you win,' admitted Rose. 'But couldn't you have parked a bit closer?'

When Hespell came round, the first thing he did was to check his own condition. Arms, then legs; nothing broken – good. He was sprawled over one of the stations on the bridge. He got carefully to his feet. The floor, although not quite horizontal, was close enough for him to stand up and orient himself. At least the ship hadn't landed upside down or on its nose. The emergency lighting was still filling the bridge with its spooky red glow, making everything look strange and dangerous.

'Are you all right, Hespell?'

It was Kendle. He should have known that the solidly built ex-marine would have survived the crash without coming to any harm.

'I'm fine, sir.'

Collins and Baker both chipped in to say that they were OK too. Which left just one person unaccounted for.

'Professor? Can you hear me?' called a concerned Hespell. 'Professor?'

'No need to shout, young man. I'm bruised and battered, but I'm not deaf. Now, can we get some proper lighting in here?'

Hespell smiled to himself. Like her reliable factotum, the professor was clearly made of strong stuff. Kendle's remarkable piloting skills had proved themselves once again. Apart from the odd cut and bruise, it transpired that none of the crew had been injured in the crash and the damage to the ship itself appeared to be minimal. Once power was back on-line, the maintenance systems would need about forty-eight hours before they could make any attempt to take off, but, all things considered, they had definitely had a lucky escape.

Kendle started to order his crew to set about the repair work, but the professor had other ideas. Now she was on the surface, Petra Shulough was already forgetting the trauma of the crash-landing and planning to explore the area.

Leaving Hespell and the others to run a full check on the condition of the ship, Shulough and Kendle left the bridge to fix the power situation. The emergency batteries were adequate to run essential systems for a few hours, but until the main trisilicate engines could be recharged an alternative power source would be needed. The professor, a firm believer in a belt-and-braces approach to any problem, had obtained a back-up power supply at their last port of call. It was still in the main cargo bay and it took a while to hook up to the ship's systems, but within half an hour it was working and the ship's central computer systems came back on-line. The professor went straight to her lab to begin testing her theory that this planet was the one she had been searching for.

Kendle watched carefully as the professor hunched over her computer, her face fixed as she studied the data from various scans. He had known Petra Shulough all her life and was well aware of just how much time and energy she had put into this search. He knew she must be excited to finally be on the surface of the planet she had dreamed about for so long, but there was no sign of it on her face. As ever, she was the picture of calm professionalism, her face set and determined.

'The kids handled that well,' he commented, as the professor scrolled through the incoming data.

'Hmm?' she muttered, not really paying him any attention.

'I said your youngsters coped with the emergency rather well.'

'They're not "my" youngsters,' she responded coolly. 'They're my crew.'

Kendle grinned. 'You can't fool me – isn't that why you wanted such a young crew, so you could mother them?' he asked.

'They were cheap,' insisted the professor frostily, and returned her full attention to the screen, ignoring Kendle's teasing.

'This is it,' she confirmed, her voice as level as ever.

'Are you sure?' he asked, but even as he spoke, he knew it was a rhetorical question. Petra Shulough would never have made the claim unless she was certain.

'No doubt in my mind. It'll take some time to prove it for sure, but this is the Paradise Planet. This is Laylora.'

Rose and the Doctor were enjoying their walk through

the forest. The plume of smoke had now blown clean away and, if it hadn't been for the way the Doctor kept taking readings on the sonic screwdriver every five minutes, Rose might have forgotten again why they were here.

'This way,' said the Doctor, slipping the device back into his pocket.

'Is there anything the sonic screwdriver can't do?' wondered Rose.

The Doctor looked a little hurt. 'Plenty. But it's still pretty useful.'

Rose shrugged. She didn't want to argue; she'd only been teasing him. She looked around again at the amazing forest that they were walking through.

'It's just perfect, isn't it?' she commented, as they passed yet another display of stunningly colourful flowers. She stopped to smell them and had to gasp at the powerful sweet odour they gave off. 'Doctor?'

The Doctor was already walking on and Rose ran to catch him up, but he stopped suddenly and she had to skid to avoid crashing into his back.

'Now what…' she began, but then she stopped as she saw what he was looking at. 'Wow!'

'Double wow!' agreed the Doctor.

In front of them, partly hidden by the trees and the undergrowth, was a collection of ruined buildings. There were a dozen or so distinct properties in various states of decay and a few more complete buildings, in the centre of which was at least one large edifice.

'So what is it? A secret city?'

The Doctor shook his head. 'Not large enough to be a city… and these ruins don't exactly look domestic. I'd say it was some kind of religious site.'

'High priests, sacrifices, that sort of thing?'

The Doctor shot her one of his wildest grins. 'If we're lucky.'

Rose looked around, trying to see signs of life. 'Doesn't look as if anyone's at home,' she said, taking a closer look at the nearest ruin. She recalled a long-distant school trip to a medieval English castle. The remains here were in a similar state: some walls were almost complete, while others were just piles of stone. Rose tried to imagine what it would have looked like when it was new.

The Doctor was on his knees in front of a number of massive stone blocks, his black-rimmed spectacles jammed on to his face. 'Hello, hello, hello…' he muttered.

'What is it?' asked Rose, hurrying to join him.

The Doctor pointed at the base of one of the larger stones. 'See that?'

Rose still couldn't work out what it was she was meant to be looking at. The stone was sitting on one of the more spectacularly coloured flowers, crushing the stem and causing the head to lie on the ground. 'What? The squashed flower?' she replied, doubt clear in her voice.

'Exactly.'

With a sudden burst of energy the Doctor stood upright and began looking around him with a more serious expression. As he slipped his glasses back into his pocket he explained his concern. 'That flower had a head on it, which means it was alive when it was crushed.'

Rose caught on. 'So the stone fell on it recently!'

The Doctor nodded. 'This planet might not be as benevolent as we first thought.'

The tribe's elders had gathered around the Talking Stone. The massive menhir, decorated with exotic carvings, marked the traditional meeting point where all male opinions were welcome. The stone was meant to act as a mediator, but on this occasion its task was easy – everyone agreed with Brother Hugan. The earth tremor had been disturbing but no major harm had been done; however, this new event – the arrival of a boat from the sky – was something else. Despite the fact that the timing of the crashed ship's arrival did not match perfectly, everyone was sure it must be connected to the disappearance of the three youths.

'Laylora is angry. We must help her cleanse her body.'

Father Opasi shook his head. As the oldest member of the tribe, his opinion was as important as the shaman's and his wisdom was respected even if he couldn't remember anyone's name from one moment to the next any more. 'We cannot act until we know what the sky boat really is. We have had visitors from the stars before. Perhaps they have returned.'

A number of the elders nodded in agreement, but Brother Hugan looked annoyed.

'Can't you see? We have to act. The next time Laylora shakes the ground it will be worse.'

Kaylen found her mother clearing up after the earth tremor. The damage to the village had been minimal, but there was still a great deal to be done. Kaylen started gathering up washing that had been scattered from the drying lines. While she worked she glanced towards the centre of the village and the Talking Stone.

'Why aren't you at the meeting?' she wondered.

Jaelette sighed. 'They said this was a matter for the elders.'

'Just the men, though,' observed Kaylen.

'Exactly!' Her mother smiled.

'What do you think they will decide?' Kaylen asked.

Jaelette just shrugged. 'Probably the wrong thing. You know what men are like!'

Kaylen was shocked, unused to hearing her mother speak so disrespectfully about the elders of the tribe.

Jaelette noticed her expression and laughed. 'You're old enough now to have your own opinion about things,' she told her daughter. 'Haven't you ever wondered how it is that we worship our planet Laylora, who is female, but it is always men who rule?'

As a matter of fact Kaylen had often thought about

that contradiction, but she was shocked to hear the same idea expressed by her mother.

The biggest building, at the centre of the area of ruins, was a particularly impressive structure. Rose was reminded of St Paul's Cathedral in London. This was clearly in the same league. It was massive – it had taken them ten minutes, even at the Doctor's pace, to walk all the way around. The lower walls were inclined at a slight angle for about three metres and then curved sharply inwards, continuing at a less extreme angle to form a curving roof. In the middle of this roof was a tapering, wide-based tower, at the top of which was a small observation platform. From a distance Rose thought the building must look like a pointy hat, with a thick wide brim, or maybe a wedding cake decorated with a giant lighthouse.

The Doctor was in his element, fascinated by every detail. At intervals along the lower walls huge panels were carved with shapes and images, and other panels featured crude paintings. He was examining them closely, his dark-rimmed glasses giving him that geeky student look that made Rose think of Jarvis Cocker.

'Fascinating,' he murmured.

Rose wasn't so impressed. 'Matchstick men and matchstick cats and dogs,' she commented.

'And matchstick monsters?' wondered the Doctor. 'What do you make of these?' He indicated a few of the crude figures which were markedly larger than the others. The monsters seemed to have four arms.

'I thought we had an emergency to attend to?' Rose reminded him.

The Doctor jumped up, whipping his glasses off. 'Of course – you're right. Now, which way is it?'

Rose looked around and realised that their detour into the ruins had caused them to lose their bearings. The forest looked pretty much the same whichever way they turned.

Even the Doctor's unerring sense of direction was letting him down. 'I think it's that way.' He indicated a direction with a vague wave of his arm.

'Are you sure?' asked Rose, doubtfully. 'We don't want to be wandering about in this forest for ever!'

The Doctor tried the sonic screwdriver again but couldn't get a clear reading. 'Something in these stones is blocking the signal,' he speculated, and then, much to Rose's surprise, he started to climb up the side of the main temple.

Fortunately, its rough stones offered plenty of purchase, and although the first three metres or so were almost straight up, after the initial stage he could clamber on to the gently sloping roof.

'I'll get a better view from up there,' the Doctor shouted back down at Rose, waving in the direction of the observation tower. 'Maybe even a clear signal. Don't wander off now...'

'As if!' muttered Rose, annoyed. She'd been travelling with the Doctor long enough now to know the dangers. Anyway, where exactly could she go?

'Oh, and hold on to this for me, can you?'

Rose looked up, but not quickly enough. The Doctor's heavy coat fell on top of her, knocking her to the ground.

'Sorry!'

Rose had struggled out from under the coat and folded it into a bundle, which she then sat on – she might as well use it for something. A nearby bush was heavy with juicy-looking red berries, which appeared to be a cross between cherries and strawberries. Rose was tempted to try one but resisted. Rules of Space-Time Travel No. 10: don't eat anything until you're sure it's totally safe. Unless it's a badly cooked kronkburger – in which case don't eat it at all.

On the roof the Doctor was now halfway between the side walls and the conical tower that formed the high point of what he was certain had to be a temple. As he got nearer, he could see that stone steps curved up around the tower, leading to the small platform at the top.

She was beginning to wonder how long the Doctor's climbing expedition would take; he seemed to have been gone an awful long time already. The sun felt quite intense. Perhaps she should have slapped on some factor 30 before leaving the TARDIS. The heat was making her feel drowsy, but as soon as she closed her eyes she heard something moving nearby. She sat up and looked around. Was it the Doctor on his way back? She stood up to gaze at the temple roof and could see the distant figure of the Doctor disappearing around the back of the tower as he climbed the spiral steps. Then she heard the sound again – somewhere behind her. She whirled around, but she couldn't see anything.

A moment ago it had been a tropical paradise, but now it was a threatening, alien environment. What was making that noise? Some kind of wild animal? Rose remembered seeing and hearing some beautiful birds during their walk, but they hadn't seen any animals. She looked around for some kind of weapon, but nothing suggested itself, unless she could throw the Doctor's coat over whatever it was.

Of course, the Doctor's coat! Rose didn't like to go through anyone's possessions, but she felt sure the Doctor would understand. She started to rummage about in the coat's enormous pockets, and straight away regretted it. Like miniature versions of the TARDIS, the Doctor's pockets seemed to go on for ever. Her fingers found an endless selection of useless stuff: a couple of yo-yos, a packet of boiled sweets, a pack of playing cards, a conker, a toy car, a banana and a cricket ball. All useless as weapons. Why couldn't she find the sonic screwdriver? OK, so she only knew about five of the 8,000 or so different settings it had, but that was better than nothing. The nearest thing she could find was a torch. Maybe whatever was out there wouldn't know the difference. Holding the torch out in front of her, she began to edge towards the sound.

It seemed to be coming from a smaller building to one side of the main temple – a long, thin structure, part of the roof of which had collapsed, with just a single entrance. Rose reached the doorway and peered through. It was gloomy and dark inside, making it hard to see anything, although a shaft of light was illuminating the far end of the space where the ceiling had caved in.

'Hello? Is anybody there?' Rose asked, trying to keep the nervous tremor out of her voice.

She could just make out a movement between the area of light and where she was standing. She took a step back and immediately tripped on the uneven floor. She fell, landing awkwardly and inelegantly on her bum. Her wrist caught on the doorway as she went down, causing the torch to fly out of her hand.

A figure appeared in the entrance. From her prone position, sprawled on her back, it looked like some kind of animal. Rose had a fleeting impression of a huge hairy body, but her eyes were drawn to the creature's hands, which terminated in shimmering talons some thirty centimetres long that were slicing through the air towards her. Closing her eyes, she threw herself to one side and, to her embarrassment, cried out in terror.

THREE

'You can keep your computers and your scans,' Kendle told Hespell solemnly, 'but if you're going to put your life and the lives of others in any danger, then there is no alternative but to examine your ship yourself.'

The ex-marine didn't just mean having a quick walk round to check that everything was in order; he meant a proper fingertip examination of the entire exterior of the ship. Which was why they had spent the last two hours on the job and had only managed to cover about a third of the ship's external surface. So far all the damage they had found was merely cosmetic, nothing that could cause any problem when they returned to space, but they had yet to approach the crucial areas at the rear, where the propulsion units were to be found. Damage to them would be a more serious matter and, as they moved slowly but inevitably towards them, it was clear that both Kendle and Hespell knew it.

'Do you think she'll fly?' Hespell asked, trying to sound casual.

Kendle answered without taking his eyes from the heat-shield panels he was examining. 'Computer says she will.'

Hespell tutted, frustrated at the answer. 'But you said we shouldn't listen to the computer,' he complained.

Kendle was about three metres away from the junior pilot and it was impossible to see his face, but Hespell just knew that the older man was grinning now when he responded. 'Yeah, I did, didn't I?'

Hespell stopped to wipe the sweat from his eyes. Although it was incredibly frustrating, he was secretly pleased that Kendle was teasing him like this; he knew it was a sign that the older man had a degree of respect for him. Hespell had seen the way Kendle treated young officers he didn't like. He seemed to have a soft spot for Baker, but Collins was always getting the sharp end of the ex-marine's tongue.

Hespell looked out towards the forest that was surrounding them. The forced landing had knocked over a number of trees and created the clearing they now rested in, but beyond that the forest was thick and dense on all sides. He felt a sudden chill as he realised that the foliage he was looking at was moving. Was it the wind?

'Sir?'

Kendle picked up the hint of alarm in the younger man's voice. 'What is it?'

Hespell raised an arm and pointed in the direction of the movement. 'There's something out there...'

Kendle slid down to join him and studied the section of forest that Hespell had indicated. 'Some kind of animal?' he speculated.

Even as he spoke the truth was revealed. It was a massive four-armed figure, covered in thick black hair like a gorilla, but this was no ape. It stood upright on powerful legs and moved with speed and purpose. Each of the four 'arms' ended in a massive paw, from the back of which long, sharp talons emerged.

'Looks like the natives might not be friendly,' muttered Kendle, bundling the younger man towards the nearest airlock and cursing the fact that he was outside on an unknown planet without any form of weapon. A rookie mistake. One that might yet prove fatal. How could he have let the professor's description of this place as a paradise lull him into such a false sense of security?

Kendle risked a quick backwards glance to see how much time they had and instantly wished he hadn't. The creature was not alone; there were two more of them. Hespell had reached the airlock and was already inside. Kendle put on an extra burst of speed, painfully aware of his age. No matter how fit he kept, it was not the same as regular combat and at times like this he had to admit that he really wasn't young any more. Gasping for breath, he reached the airlock and all but fell into the chamber. Instantly Hespell hit the controls and the outer doors slammed shut with a hydraulic hiss. Kendle took a moment to recover, while Hespell opened the inner doors and reached for the intercom.

'All hands, we are under attack from native life forms. Seal the ship!' he shouted.

In her quarters Professor Shulough reacted to the intercom announcement with annoyance. How frustrating. Native life forms. That was something she hadn't allowed for. Of course she knew the Paradise Planet was inhabited – she'd read the personal account of the explorer who had first stumbled across the place fifty years ago – but the inhabitants were meant to be peaceful humanoids, not wild monsters. Was it possible that this wasn't the right planet after all?

The professor went back to reviewing her evidence, but was interrupted by a knock at the door. It opened to reveal Kendle, looking older and somehow frailer than she had ever seen him.

'Professor, we may have to make a rapid departure.'

'No.' She was adamant. 'We're not leaving.'

'Haven't you heard? We're under attack!' Kendle insisted with his usual authority.

'Then do your job,' the professor threw back at him. 'You're meant to be a soldier, aren't you? Defend us.'

Rose was certain that the next thing she felt would be sharp pain as those vicious talons sliced into her and she just hoped they wouldn't cut anything too vital – like a major blood vessel! Eyes squeezed tight shut, she kept rolling from side to side, but the fatal blow never came.

'It's OK, you're safe! Stop rolling around.'

It was the monster – only it didn't sound very monsterish. In fact, it sounded like a young man. Gingerly Rose opened her eyes. The 'monster' was trying to pull its own head off. With a final effort it succeeded and Rose realised that the 'head' was, in fact, nothing more than a mask. It wasn't a monster at all but someone in a monster costume! And now Rose knew the truth, she could see that it wasn't even a very good monster costume. The hairy legs of the beast stopped about thirty centimetres above the ground, revealing a pair of athletic-looking humanoid legs. And where the fearsome monster's head had been, a much more attractive human head was sticking out of the monster's shoulders. Rose thought it looked like someone sticking their face through one of those comedy photo opportunity boards you find at seaside resorts, the ones that let you have your photo taken with the cartoon body of some fat beach-lover. The clawed paws were merely gloves, which were quickly shrugged off.

'I'm sorry. I didn't mean to scare you,' said the youth inside the monster costume, smiling.

Rose instantly relaxed. When it came to men, she really was her mother's daughter – a nice smile took a bloke a long way, and this lad had a really nice smile. His hair, short and spiky, was a sun-dyed blond and his skin glowed with a healthy tan that had nothing to do with a bottle. Perfect blue eyes and teeth that would make an orthodontist proud completed the look. Rose allowed herself to be helped up.

'You're like me!' he exclaimed, clearly surprised.

Rose blushed, still embarrassed by the way she'd reacted to his arrival. Had she really screamed?

'Well, I guess I have my blonde moments, if that's what you mean.'

The boy – Rose would have guessed his age at around seventeen – shook his head. 'No, no…' He reached a hand towards her head and she resisted the instinct to flinch. He gently brushed the hair away from her face and with hesitant fingers stroked the top of her ear. Rose gave an involuntary shiver. 'You're like me,' he repeated. 'The same race.'

'Human,' Rose whispered, 'you're human.'

The boy looked into her eyes and smiled a grateful smile.

'My name's Rose,' she stuttered, suddenly nervous, feeling as if she'd just approached a shy lad at a club and asked him to dance when she should simply have introduced herself first. Feeling terribly self-conscious she offered him her hand.

'Rez,' offered the boy by way of reply. Instinctively he took her proffered hand but, not knowing what to do with it, just held it.

'You're meant to shake,' explained Rose kindly.

A frown flittered across the blond boy's face and then he started to shake his entire body. Rose didn't want to be cruel, but it was such a funny sight that she couldn't stop the laughter bursting out.

Her new friend started laughing too. Soon the pair of them were helpless, leaning against each other for support, the discarded monster costume forgotten at their feet.

The screen was filled with static. Moments before, it had given the entire bridge an uncomfortably close-up image of one of the creatures as the sharp-looking talons sliced towards the security camera, but now it showed nothing.

'That thing just took out the camera. But that's impossible,' exclaimed Hespell. 'It must have cut straight through the metal!'

'Imagine what it would do to you,' Kendle muttered.

'Where are they?' It was the professor, who had reluctantly joined them on the bridge, concerned that the attack might adversely affect her own mission.

'Climbing over the hull.'

'Can they get through it?'

Kendle shrugged. 'If they can slice through metal, the hull won't hold them for long.'

'There must be something we can do. Doesn't this ship have any defence capabilities? I thought it had seen military service.'

'You wanted a ship suitable for exploring. You never said you wanted to wage war!' replied Kendle.

'I didn't know I'd need to.'

Kendle looked around the room. The crew were all

young and raw. Right now he'd have welcomed just one more face like his own, one with the scars of experience on it, but none of these kids looked like they'd lived at all. And if he couldn't find a way of stopping the current attack, none of them would live much longer. He racked his brain, trying to think of something he could do.

'Metal, metal…' he muttered. Of course. 'The hull is metal, isn't it?'

It took Hespell a moment to realise that Kendle was talking to him. 'Yes, sir.'

'And the emergency generator is running at full power?'

Hespell nodded, then looked shocked when he understood what Kendle was suggesting. 'You want me to electrify the hull?'

The other man met his gaze. 'Is it possible?'

Hespell sucked his teeth, considering. 'It's certainly possible, in theory, but in practice… It'll fry a lot of our sensors.'

'Sensors can be replaced, people can't. Do it.'

It took a few minutes of frantic work by every member of the crew. Sensitive systems had to be off-lined and isolated and conductive wires connected between the generator and the hull. While the minutes ticked away, they were all conscious of the sounds echoing through the ship's corridors, as the creatures crawled over the hull, apparently trying to find a way in. The hull creaked and groaned eerily, as everyone hurried to complete the necessary circuit. They worked in a tense silence that was occasionally punctuated by the screech of tearing metal. The creatures seemed determined to get inside the ship.

Finally they were ready. Kendle gave the order and Hespell flicked the switch, sending a massive current through the hull.

The sounds from the hull ceased.

The silence held for a long moment, then Kendle gave the order to shut off the current. 'Do we have any cameras working?' he demanded.

Hespell nodded and flicked a switch.

On the screen they could see that their desperate measure had produced the desired result. The creatures had been hurled metres away from the hull by the electrical force. The three of them were lying on the ground, their fur smoking slightly. But incredibly, as the crew watched in horror, they staggered to their feet again and began shuffling towards the ship.

'Power up,' ordered Kendle.

Hespell quickly reactivated the current. The viewscreen picture crackled with interference but it was still possible to see what was happening. One of the creatures made another attempt to climb on to the ship, but the electrified hull sent him flying backwards. Eventually, having been thwarted in their efforts, the trio turned and headed back into the forest. For now...

Kendle watched as the three enormous beasts

disappeared and then got to his feet purposefully. 'Hespell, Collins, with me,' he ordered.

Hespell and the usually cool Jae Collins exchanged nervous looks. Kendle noticed their reluctance and offered them a further explanation.

'We're going after them,' he said. 'In my experience, attack is always the best form of defence.'

The Doctor was sorry now that he had left Rose at ground level. Not because he wanted her to have the same aching legs that he had after climbing to the summit of the tower, but because he really wanted to share the wonderful view with her. This was one of the reasons why he travelled, to see incredible things, and it just wasn't the same if he couldn't share the experience with someone else.

The view from the observation post was absolutely breathtaking. He could see for miles in every direction and each point of the compass offered a stunning vista. This planet truly was a beautiful place, but it was more than just a visual thing; it *felt* wonderful too. The Doctor couldn't be sure exactly what it was. Perhaps the gravity which was just slightly less than Earth's. Perhaps it was the atmosphere, which seemed to have a little more oxygen in it. Or perhaps it was simply one of those feel-good planets you found now and then where everything was just right. For a brief moment his mind went back to the planet he had grown up on, so many years ago. That had been one of those perfect planets. All gone now. Dust to dust. The Doctor shook his head to scatter the ghosts haunting his thoughts and returned his attention to the present. Emergency distress call, he reminded himself, crashed spaceship.

He started scanning the horizon for signs of the ship's descent. They weren't hard to find. The ship had damaged a strip of forest as it came in to make what had clearly been a poor landing, and this acted like a giant arrow pointing to the crash site. Even at this distance the Doctor could see that the spaceship was still essentially intact. With luck there would have been no fatalities.

Making a mental note of the direction he would need to take, the Doctor began the long trip back to ground level. As he skipped down the stairs, taking care not to go too fast for fear of losing his footing on the worn stone steps, he continued to cast glances out towards the crashed spaceship. Was that movement he could see? Something crashing through the forest from the landing site and moving towards the ruins? The Doctor had a sudden bad feeling and increased his pace, desperate now to get back to Rose. He reached the bottom of the steps and began the more difficult part of the descent, along the sloping roof. On the way up this had been easy, but coming down gravity made it far more treacherous and the Doctor wanted to arrive in one piece.

Kendle led the way, every inch the soldier now, plasma

rifle cocked and ready in his hands. Hespell and Collins followed, looking less comfortable with their own weapons. Kendle was using all his old tracking skills to follow the creatures that had attacked them, but it wasn't a particularly difficult task. The powerful beasts had raced through the forest, breaking branches and undergrowth just like two-legged bulldozers. Even Hespell could see where they had been. At least he could when the forest was quite dense, but now that the trees were thinning out the trail was becoming less obvious.

Kendle, who had been leading them at a brisk trot, waved a hand to slow them down. Up ahead was a clearing in which some stone buildings, most of them in a ruinous state, could be seen. Of the creatures there was now no sign. Using what cover they could find, the three humans crept closer to the ruins.

Collins and Hespell looked at each other – both were feeling increasingly anxious about this course of action. Following Kendle in the forest had been one thing, but now they felt much more exposed. The further they went into the ruins, the greater the risk of the creatures circling round and attacking them from the rear.

The sun was now quite low in the sky and cast long shadows on all sides, making the place seem even eerier. In the centre of the clearing was a large building with an impressive tower built on top of its roof. Kendle seemed to be taking them towards it. Was it the creatures' lair? A movement on the lower part of the roof caught Hespell's eye. Had one of the creatures been watching their progress? Instinctively he raised his weapon and took aim.

The Doctor was nearly on the ground and was about to call out to Rose when he saw the humans. They were creeping through the undergrowth, dashing between piles of stone and bushes, taking up defensive positions. He could see that they were armed and their movements suggested that they were expecting trouble. Which could be bad news for any strangers they might encounter. Trigger-happy humans were, in the Doctor's experience, the worst kind of humans. He had to get down there quickly and defuse the situation before anyone got sh –

The Doctor never finished his thought. A blast from one of the soldiers hit him, stunning him instantly. He staggered and fell before rolling down the incline and toppling over the lip at the part where the wall became almost vertical.

If Rez hadn't clamped his hand over her mouth, Rose would have cried out. Rez had taken her to the storeroom in which he had found the monster costume. It was down some earthen steps, in a cellar. All sorts of ceremonial costumes and props were stored there. 'Like some kind of weird dressing-up box,' Rose had commented. Rez had shown her his other recent discovery. Hidden behind a tapestry that was hanging on the wall was a tunnel.

'Where does it lead?' she had asked.

Rez had shrugged and given her one of his trademark grins. 'There are loads of tunnels and cellars under the ruins. Shall we explore?' He had offered his hand and for a moment she was temped to go with him; something in his manner made her think of another adventurous spirit – the Doctor. But then she realised that she couldn't go anywhere until the Doctor got back. She had explained about her friend and how he would be worried about her. Rez had been disappointed, perhaps even a bit jealous at the news that Rose already had a male companion, but he quickly hid his disappointment and led her back the way they had come. As they reached the doorway, Rez had suddenly stopped and indicated that she should be quiet. Rose frowned – what was the problem? She squeezed next to him in the doorway – not an entirely unpleasant act – and looked out in the same direction. Across the ruins, she saw what looked like another human, but this one was dressed in some kind of uniform and, more worryingly, was carrying a weapon.

Rose figured out instinctively that shouting a cheery hello would be the wrong move right now. The best thing was to watch and wait. Suddenly the red-headed man with the gun was reacting to something above eye level. He raised his weapon. A cold dread hit Rose in the stomach. She had a sudden awful feeling about what was happening in front of her. She was about to shout a warning, but that was when Rez had grabbed her. Rose watched helplessly as the man fired a blast and a moment later the unconscious figure of the Doctor rolled off the roof and fell to the ground. Ironically his own coat, lying where Rose had left it, broke his fall.

Two other humans, also armed, joined the man who had shot at the Doctor. Rose and Rez watched as the three strangers had a hushed conversation. The Doctor's face was turned towards them and suddenly his eyes flicked open. Rose felt the Doctor looking directly at her. As she watched he gave her a deliberate wink and then closed his eyes again. He's playing possum, she thought to herself. And he wants me to go along with it.

The oldest of the three strangers, who looked to be in charge, checked the Doctor and, satisfied with his condition, ordered the other two to pick him and his coat up. With a last quick look around the ruins, the leader led his two juniors and their stunned captive away.

'You should have let me do something,' Rose exploded as soon as she could speak. 'They shot the Doctor!'

'What are you suggesting we should have done? Thrown rocks at them?'

He had a point. It was clear that the pair of them

wouldn't have had a hope against the three, armed men.

'They must have come from the crashed spaceship,' Rose decided. 'And now he's letting them take him there. But he's expecting me to follow. I'm sure he is…'

Rez shook his head firmly.

'I can't just let him go,' Rose told him angrily.

'It's getting dark. The forest is dangerous at night. We'll find your friend at the crash site in the morning. I promise.'

Rose could see that Rez was being practical, but that didn't mean she had to like it.

'So what happens till then?'

Rez considered for a moment before taking her hand and leading her away. 'I'll take you to the village. You'll be safe there.'

FOUR

As she followed her new friend through the rapidly darkening forest, Rose tried to keep calm and not worry about the Doctor. She knew the weapon had just stunned him – he'd been pretending to be unconscious when the two men started to carry him away. If only she knew what the wink had meant. Was it just an 'I'm OK' wink or did it mean something else? Was the Doctor expecting her to follow him straight away? Whatever it meant, morning would come soon enough, and Rose was confident that she would catch up with him then. In the meantime, perhaps she should learn a little more about where she was.

'So what's this place called?' she asked, as Rez helped her over a fallen tree.

'Laylora,' he told her.

It was a beautiful name for a beautiful planet, and when Rose said as much he smiled.

'Laylora provides,' he replied, in the same way that old ladies said, 'God bless you!' back home, with an automatic but simple reverence.

Rose noticed that the trees were thinning out and it wasn't long before they reached the edge of the forest. In front of them was an undulating plain, scattered with odd clumps of trees but mostly given over to abundant wild grass. Nestled in a hollow, in the shadow of some small hills, was a settlement. At first glance it looked like a campsite and then, as they drew closer, Rose got a slightly different feeling. It was familiar but for a moment she couldn't work out why. Then it hit her – it was a bit like a Native American village, the sort that she'd seen in the movies. Mickey had a bunch of classic Hollywood Westerns on DVD and he'd made Rose sit through a few. They hadn't really appealed to her, although Kevin Costner wasn't bad-looking for a bloke his age, but she had been interested in the odd glimpses of the lifestyle that had been featured. And it was that Native American feeling that she was getting now.

The Laylorans were all dressed in simple but colourful clothes and lived in large, tent-like buildings. Fires burned in front of each individual dwelling and a much larger fire could be seen in the middle of the village, where there was a sort of public space. Large human-sized stones with intricate carvings were placed at various points around the village. Rose couldn't help but see them as granite totem poles. The tents themselves were made from animal skins sewn together, then draped over complex wooden frames. They were more like the modern camping tents Rose had seen in the Argos catalogue than the classic pointy-roofed tepees, but she didn't mind that. The fact that she could find something familiar in this alien location was a comfort, and Rose needed all the comforts she could get right now.

Their arrival had caused a bit of a stir. Rose had been introduced to a flurry of people, none of whose names stuck in her head for a moment. The Laylorans were rather excitable; apparently it had been quite a day – not only had there been the shock of the spaceship crashing, but they had also suffered a mammoth earth tremor. And now Rose had suddenly appeared from nowhere. But there was something else, something they weren't telling her. Rose noticed that some people were giving her intense looks and then turning away when she looked back at them. One woman had red-rimmed eyes, suggesting she had been doing a lot of crying. Had the tremor been worse than they were letting on? Had people died? Rose decided to ask Rez when they were alone again.

Everyone wanted to know whether Rose had come from the crashed sky boat. She tried to explain that she'd arrived by other means but wasn't sure she should tell them about the TARDIS. She didn't want them carting it off and making it an offering to their precious Laylora. She'd picked up the idea that these people saw the planet as a goddess and she knew what that meant. Like she had said to the Doctor: sacrifices. Rose realised that she had to tread carefully. No matter how familiar these people might seem, she had to remember that they were *not* displaced Native Americans. If she upset them, she might suffer a much worse fate than being scalped.

Rez led her through the crowd to a particular tent, where she was introduced to his adopted mother, Jaelette, who instantly gathered her into a warm hug. Jaelette was a short, plump Layloran with a kind face and she reminded Rose of her own mother, although to be fair Jackie had never been quite this maternal. Jaelette studied Rose carefully and then looked at Rez with sad eyes. Before she could say anything, a girl who seemed to be a couple of years older than Rose appeared from within the tent. The newcomer rushed to envelop Rez in a huge bear hug, completely ignoring Rose.

'Where have you been?' the girl demanded, when she finally allowed him to breathe. 'I was so worried.'

Rez looked a bit sheepish. 'I was clearing up at the temple, like you suggested. And then I ran into...' He stopped, seeing the expression on his sister's face. 'Er, this is Rose,' he continued, changing tack. 'Rose this is Kaylen, my sister.'

Not his girlfriend, then. Not, she told herself quickly, that she'd mind if he did have a girlfriend; she and the Doctor were here on a mission of mercy, not on the pull, but it might have been awkward if this

Kaylen had been his girlfriend, that's all. However, by the look on the young Layloran woman's face, it might still be a problem.

'She's like you!' exclaimed Kaylen, and there was an odd mixture of surprise and sadness in her voice.

What did she mean, like him? Was this a blonde thing? Rose realised that most of the Laylorans did have dark-coloured hair, but she was sure that wasn't what Kaylen was getting at. And then she noticed the girl's hand, which was grasping Rez's arm. She had only three fingers. Three fingers and a thumb. And her other hand was the same.

Now, as she looked more closely, Rose could see that all the Laylorans had the same number of fingers. And once she started really looking at them, she saw that there were more things marking them out as alien rather than human. They had rounder eyes and flatter noses and their ears were gently pointed. Not total Spock jobs, but more like the classic elf look. No wonder Rez had checked out her ears when they had first met. They might not be as weird-looking as the Moxx of Balhoon or the Ood, but these *were* aliens!

'I don't understand... You're human, but they're not, is that right?' she asked Rez.

'We found him when he was a baby. In a little sky boat,' explained Jaelette.

Rose nodded. Just like Superman, but without all the super-strength and X-ray vision, she thought to herself.

'But didn't anyone come looking for you?' she asked. 'You must have come from somewhere…'

Rez shrugged. 'I don't know.'

Rose persisted. 'Somewhere out there someone must know who you are, where you come from. You might have relatives, parents…'

'The tribe are my family now,' Rez told her solemnly.

'Brother Hugan will want to see her,' Kaylen said, interrupting their discussion.

Rez nodded and led Rose towards a large tent that was more gaudily decorated than most. 'Brother Hugan is our shaman,' he explained, so Rose wasn't surprised when the tent flap was pulled back and an extraordinarily attired Layloran appeared.

He was one of the oldest natives she had seen up to now, with skin so weathered by the years that it looked like leather. As well as the simple tunic and loose-fitting three-quarter-length trousers that most of the males wore, Brother Hugan also sported a heavy-looking ceremonial cloak of vibrant colours that made Rose think of Philip Schofield playing Joseph on her mum's CD of the *Technicolor Dreamcoat*. On his head the shaman had some kind of animal-skin headdress, decorated with bird feathers. To complete the look his face was decorated with stripes of make-up and a heavily jewelled necklace hung around his neck. In fact, Rose now realised, a lot of the Laylorans were wearing jewellery, and most of the bracelets, anklets and necklaces seemed to have large and, to her mind, ostentatious gemstones and crystals in them.

'Laylora is angry,' announced the shaman, his fierce expression amplified by the war paint. 'She will call forth the Witiku! We must prepare ourselves.'

'Witiku? What the hell are they?' queried Rose.

'Laylora's protectors,' Kaylen offered by way of explanation.

Rez must have realised that this was a bit short on detail, because he leaned close to whisper in her ear. 'They're mythical monsters that appear when Laylora is threatened. There are pictures of them all over the temple. That costume I was wearing is meant to represent them.'

Rose didn't like the sound of this. The costume hadn't been that frightening once she'd realised that a human being was inside it, but the idea of a real creature like that was something else.

Brother Hugan was speaking again. 'Our ancestors knew how to keep Laylora happy. We have forgotten too many of the old ways,' he announced.

Rose felt a shiver of apprehension. She didn't like the direction things were going in. Suddenly she was very aware that she was in the middle of an alien settlement, surrounded by aliens. And that she was alone.

'We have become lazy in our devotions,' continued the shaman, looking around at the people of the tribe.

'There is only one way to placate Laylora's wrath. We must make her an offering…'

An offering? What was he going to do – hand round a collection plate?

In the silence that followed, Rose began to get a nasty feeling that the old man had something a bit more drastic in mind.

'We must offer her a sacrifice!'

The gathered Laylorans reacted with mutters and gasps, but Brother Hugan simply responded by raising his voice even louder.

'Laylora provides,' he screamed.

And automatically the Laylorans all responded in kind. 'Laylora provides,' they chanted.

'Laylora provides,' the shaman cried again, louder still.

And this time the response from the crowd was deafening.

It's getting a bit like a rock concert, thought Rose. He'll have them singing the chorus in a minute.

'Laylora provides,' Brother Hugan screeched for a third time. 'But Laylora demands of us in return!'

This time the crowd stayed silent.

'Laylora demands a blood sacrifice!'

Rose swallowed hard. Blood sacrifice! She didn't like the sound of that. She looked around and realised, with a shiver of dread, that all the Laylorans were staring at her.

Brother Hugan wanted to offer his precious living

planet a sacrifice and he appeared to have already chosen her for the honour.

FIVE

The problem with being in a very small crew, Hespell decided, was that there weren't enough junior ranks to assign all the really tedious jobs to. So even being second pilot (well, technically trainee pilot, not that anyone seemed to be taking his training very seriously on this mission) was no protection against a spell of duty as notional 'security officer'. Of course, most of the time the ship didn't need a security officer, so the extra duty hadn't been a problem. But now... Now they had a prisoner and someone had to guard him. Hespell thought he had definitely drawn the short straw.

He sighed and shifted in his seat. He'd been here for what seemed like hours, watching the prisoner do absolutely nothing. The stun charge the man had been hit with should have ceased to have any effect by now, but he still seemed to be out cold. Hespell wondered how much longer he would have to wait.

'Not much of a cell, is it?'

He nearly fell off his chair. The prisoner was awake. Fully awake, when a moment ago he'd appeared to be dead to the world, completely unconscious.

'I'm sorry,' he muttered, utterly wrong-footed.

'Oh, it's nothing to apologise for. I've seen worse. In fact, by most standards this is pretty cosy. Just not very cell-like, that's all.'

The prisoner was sitting up now, looking around the cabin with curious eyes. He winked cheerfully at his guard and carried on examining his surroundings.

'It's not actually a cell, you see...' Hespell started to explain. 'It's my cabin.'

'I'm being held prisoner in someone's bedroom?'

'We... er... don't really have anywhere else.'

'A ship this size? That's odd.'

'Decks three, four and five are mothballed,' Hespell told him. 'We're a small crew.'

The prisoner considered this for a moment and then nodded. 'Fair enough. I won't complain if you don't. I'm the Doctor, by the way...' And with that he was on his feet. 'I'd shake your hand, but I'm a bit tied up,' he added, indicating his bound wrists.

Hespell actually found himself reaching forward to untie the man when he remembered the nature of their relationship and brought his weapon up to bear on the stranger.

'Trainee Pilot Hespell,' he offered a little lamely.

'Pleased to meet you, I'm sure,' said the Doctor, beaming. 'There's really no need for that, you know,' he added, gently pushing the barrel of the weapon away from him. 'I'm not dangerous.'

Hespell had to admit the man didn't look very dangerous. He seemed to be in his early thirties, dressed in a classic pinstriped two-piece suit, the kind that had been in and out of fashion for centuries. A rather scruffy tie was loosely knotted around the neck of his white shirt and a pair of casual sneakers were on his feet. Definitely not dangerous.

'I guess you don't look much like the monsters. But I didn't know that when I shot you...' Hespell allowed himself to look a little embarrassed. 'Sorry about that.'

The Doctor smiled again. 'Not to worry. No permanent damage done.'

Hespell was relieved. He didn't like the idea of shooting anyone, and certainly not someone who was as reasonable as this.

'So what was that about monsters, then?' asked the man casually.

And Hespell was so beguiled by the stranger's charm that he found himself talking.

The Doctor listened carefully to his account of the attack by the creatures, interrupting occasionally to ask the odd question. When Hespell had finished the Doctor sat back on the bunk and threw his still-tied hands behind his head.

'Interesting,' he commented simply.

Hespell couldn't quite believe his ears. Interesting! 'Actually, it was pretty frightening to be honest.'

'Running away from monsters? You get used to it after a while.' The Doctor flashed another quick smile, but his eyes remained serious. 'So tell me, what exactly are you doing on this planet?'

'If you wouldn't mind – that's one question I'd like to hear your answer to.'

A new voice had joined the conversation. Hespell realised that Kendle had appeared in the doorway without making a sound – his marine training in action again. Kendle glared at the Doctor, his face revealing nothing. Hespell bit his lip in anticipation: this was a confrontation that looked as if it might be very entertaining.

'Hello,' said the Doctor brightly. 'And who are you?'

Rose looked around at the locals, who had her surrounded on all sides. They seemed to be lapping up everything the old man was saying. Were they really thinking of sacrificing her?

Before the shaman could make any further move towards that end, Rez stepped out of the crowd, holding his hands up.

'Wait!' he called out. 'Just hold on a minute.'

Now everyone was looking at Rez.

He took a deep breath and then addressed the crowd. 'Is this how Laylora wants us to treat our visitors? With suspicion and hatred and a violent death?'

As Rez spoke, he moved subtly to take up a position

between Rose and the shaman. Again Rose could see a hint of the Doctor in her new friend – it was exactly the sort of thing he would have done.

Rez looked around at his adopted people, meeting as many pairs of eyes as he could. 'When I came here, as a baby, you welcomed me and took me into your homes. Why is this arrival any different?'

There was an awkward silence and for a moment Rose wasn't sure which way things were going to go. But then the moment broke and the mood of the crowd changed. With most of the men away, the women were in the majority and few of them had any great appetite for blood sacrifice.

Brother Hugan could sense it too. 'I didn't mean we should sacrifice the girl,' he explained, hurriedly backtracking. 'But we must appease Laylora in some way.'

'Whatever you think we need to do, whatever ritual must be performed, I'll help,' Rez told him. 'But killing Rose isn't going to do anything for anyone.'

'Rez is right,' Mother Jaelette's voice rang out. 'Brother Hugan did not mean to frighten Rose, did you?'

The shaman shook his head. 'Of course not.' He looked Rose in the eye and added, 'I'm sorry.'

Despite everything Rose felt some sympathy for the old man. A moment ago he had seemed so important and vital to the village and now he looked like a joke.

'I will perform the Ritual of Understanding,' Brother

Hugan announced, with as much dignity as he could muster, and disappeared into his tent.

The crowd broke up, drifting off in various directions, leaving Rez and Rose standing alone.

'Thanks,' Rose said simply.

'Any time,' replied Rez, a little shyly. 'Would you like something to eat?'

Now he mentioned food, Rose realised that she was very hungry. She smiled broadly at him. 'You know what, I think I would.'

'Who is he?' Professor Shulough demanded.

Two hours had passed since Kendle had entered the temporary cell and she was impatient to hear the results. Kendle just shrugged, a bemused expression on his lined face.

'I've interrogated hundreds of prisoners in my time and I've never come up against one like this,' he explained.

The professor was surprised to hear such a defeated tone in her old friend's voice. 'You can't get him to talk?'

'Actually, I can't get him to shut up!'

She frowned, wrong-footed. 'I don't understand.'

'He just keeps blithering on... That man could talk for the Empire. He just won't stop,' complained Kendle.

'So has he told you who he is and what he wants here?'

'I wish.'

Frustrated, the professor started to pace the corridor. 'We have to know what he's doing here.'

Kendle glanced back into the cabin where the man was still being held.

The professor came up alongside him. 'Maybe I should have a go…'

Rose had to smile. The more she travelled with the Doctor, the more unexpected life became. If someone had told her this morning that she'd end the day having dinner with a fit-looking lad a few years her junior – in a tent, no less – she'd have laughed in their face. For a start, camping was just *so* not her. Rose and some friends from school had tried it once, at a summer rock festival. It had been a laugh the first night, but two more days of having to get up and walk a kilometre through the mud in the middle of the night to use the loo had soon lost its appeal. That would have been bad enough, but then they'd had to deal with more rainfall in forty-eight hours than England had seen in the previous two months. After that experience Rose had sworn that she'd never spend a night 'under canvas' again.

And yet here she was… on a date with the original Mr Back-to-Nature. Rez had led her away from the Talking Stone to a small tent that was situated a little way to the side of the larger tent belonging to Mother Jaelette.

'Last year I was allowed to move into my own space,' he had explained, opening the tent flap to allow her to enter.

Inside it was simply furnished with woven rugs and furs. Rose had half-expected him to go and fetch some food from his stepmother next door, but he surprised her by starting to prepare a meal himself.

She watched as he stirred the contents of a saucepan, which was suspended over the fire in front of his tent. The crackling flames threw interesting patterns across his chiselled features. Rose wondered what it must have been like to be brought up knowing that you were different from everyone else. Was he teased when he was younger, for not having the pointy ears or for having the extra finger? It must have been hard for him.

'Do you know much about your…' Rose hesitated, unsure what the right word was. 'About who you are and where you come from?' she continued finally, changing direction.

'My "real" parents,' he replied, still stirring rhythmically, 'that's what you were going to say, wasn't it?'

Blushing, Rose nodded.

'I know a little. There were some things packed into the escape pod I landed in, some keepsakes: a weird cube thing…' He trailed off and concentrated on ladling the broth from the saucepan into two bowls.

'I'm sorry,' murmured Rose, as he passed her one of the bowls.

'It's OK, really,' Rez assured her, coming to join her and sitting on the ground in the shade of the tent's awning.

Although it was now dark, it was still pleasantly warm. Rose took a tentative sip of the thick soup. Exotic but alien vegetables swam in a thick, orange-coloured liquid. Rose hoped it tasted as good as it smelt. It did. In spades.

'This is fantastic,' she gushed.

'Thank you,' he said, smiling. 'I don't make it as well as Mother Jaelette but I try…'

The Doctor looked up as the cabin door opened again. This time it was a woman, another human, but she clearly wasn't a soldier. There was an air of intelligence about her. The Doctor wondered if perhaps he might be able to get through to this one.

'I'm Professor Petra Shulough. I'm in command of this mission,' she announced by way of an opening gambit. 'I'm sorry that you've been inconvenienced like this.'

The Doctor smiled disarmingly. 'Oh, it's no trouble,' he began, 'but I could do with having my wrists untied. It's not good for the circulation, you know.'

The professor gave the prisoner a long, cool look, evaluating him. He certainly didn't seem dangerous, but she knew that didn't necessarily mean anything. Hespell watched the pair of them, his gun held at the ready.

'Mr Hespell, untie the prisoner!'

Hespell hurried to obey the order.

'It's the Doctor, actually,' the Doctor said, rubbing his freed wrists, 'and thank you.' He spied his coat lying on the bunk and picked it up. 'Thanks for this as well. You're too kind.'

'Don't be so hasty, "Doctor". One aggressive move and Mr Hespell will shoot you. And not on a stun setting this time.'

'Understood,' the Doctor said, getting to his feet. 'Now, shall we start again? I'm the Doctor. My friend Rose and I picked up your mayday signal and we're here, wherever we are, to help.'

The professor frowned. 'You've no idea where you are?'

The Doctor looked around and then back at the stern-faced woman. 'The planet? No. This ship? Well, going on the design and what I saw of it from the outside, I'd have to say it's not exactly showroom new, is it? What's the date? Some time in the late twenty-fourth century? Your ship doesn't have any serious armaments. Looks to me to be some kind of deep-space explorer.'

The Doctor stole a quick look at the professor, but her face wasn't giving away anything. Oh well, in for a penny, thought the Doctor.

'You say you're the commander, but you're not wearing a uniform, so we're not talking military expedition, are we? So… who lives in a spaceship like this? Private explorer? Mineral speculator, perhaps? Am I getting warm?'

'I am looking for something,' the professor confessed.

The Doctor's interest was piqued. 'And what would that be, then?'

'A planet called Laylora.'

The Doctor repeated the name, testing the sounds of the word in his mouth, while trying to work out if he had ever heard of the place. So many planets, so many names...

'Laylora, Laylora... *Laylora!*'

'You've heard of it?'

The Doctor nodded his head. 'Yes, I think so... It's one of those legendary worlds that may or may not exist − all half-truths and rumour. Of course, I'm probably remembering it from the future. One of the side effects of time travel...'

The professor stared at him, convinced the man was a fool, or mad, or possibly both. 'But you do recognise the name?' she demanded.

'Well, yes, I think so. A planet reputed to be perfect in every way. The Paradise Planet. But it doesn't exist, does it? It's just a myth.'

'It's no myth, Doctor,' said the professor with pride. 'This is Laylora!'

The rear doors of the bridge opened and Kendle was surprised to see Hespell stride through.

'Mr Hespell, have you left the professor alone with the prisoner?'

Hespell looked a little embarrassed. 'She insisted.'

Kendle sighed. 'Doesn't she understand – that man might be linked to those creatures that attacked us! Does she want to get herself killed?'

Hespell was smart enough to know that the older man didn't want an answer to that.

'How are the repairs to our sensor array going?' he asked, hoping that changing the subject wouldn't get him into trouble.

'Auto-repair systems are cycling through. We should have most of the video and infrared back on-line within the hour.'

Hespell nodded an acknowledgement and slipped into his seat. With power still a precious commodity, most of his console was dead, but at least he could monitor some systems to keep himself busy.

In the command chair, Kendle was deep in thought. Hespell wondered what the man was thinking. Was he really worried about the professor being left alone with the Doctor? Or was he thinking about the creatures that had attacked them, trying to come up with a strategy to deal with them the next time they met?

'Do you think they'll come back?' Hespell asked, breaking the oppressive silence.

'Of course they will.' Kendle was certain of it. 'Whatever it was they wanted they didn't get, did they?

They'll be back all right.'

Hespell laughed nervously. 'So much for paradise!'

Jae Collins was stuck. He had been dispatched to oversee the environmental systems, the control matrix for which had been damaged in the crash. He found the various controls a mess of burnt-out circuit boards and broken connections.

With a heavy heart he had begun to take various parts of the system off-line when a power outage had locked the doors to the room. He tried to call for help via the intercom, but it too had ceased to function.

After a half-hearted attempt to pull open the doors manually, Collins slumped to the floor. Why, oh why, had he ever volunteered for this ridiculous mission? The first time he'd seen the banged-up *Humphrey Bogart* he knew he'd made a terrible mistake. And yet he had still joined up.

His fellow crewmates were fresh academy graduates with stars in their eyes, the ship's owner was a steel-hearted obsessive and the pilot was an old soldier looking for one more fight. Every instinct had told Collins that joining this crew was a bad idea. The problem was, he didn't have a choice. He needed to drop out of sight. Unfinished business with the banks that had funded his space-yacht-racing career and gambling debts that would bankrupt a small planet all added up to an urgent need to get out of his home system and vanish.

The offer of a place on board the *Humphrey Bogart* had seemed like a lifesaver. Now he feared it might yet cost him his life.

Collins's nose wrinkled – something was burning. That's all he needed. He looked up at the ceiling, at the nozzles from which nothing was shooting. The fire sprinklers must be off-line too. Great!

'Be careful. It's very old.'

The Doctor smiled to himself. So you do care about some things, he thought.

Professor Shulough had taken him to her quarters to explain about her quest. She told him about how she had amassed a large collection of clues and evidence relating to Laylora and its location, the most valuable of which was the book he was now examining – a handwritten journal. The yellowing pages were crisp and fragile and the Doctor had to take care as he flicked through not to inflict any further damage.

Reading at a speed no human could match, the Doctor scanned the pages, taking in huge amounts of information. It was an old-fashioned diary, the personal record of someone called Maurit Guillan.

'Guillan was an explorer working for one of the big corporations back home. His ship was on a long-term survey mission, looking for suitable planets,' the professor explained.

The Doctor paused in his speed-reading and shot her a cool look. With his glasses perched on his nose, he looked quite severe, but it was all water off a duck's back to the professor.

'Suitable for what? Strip-mining of all its mineral assets?' he suggested icily.

'The Empire doesn't run on air, Doctor. Things have to be built, raw materials have to come from somewhere. The Empire always needs new planets for expansion, colonisation, exploitation…'

'So having ravaged your own world and made it little better than a giant rubbish-filled quarry, now you're looking to do the same to other worlds, is that it?'

The professor was quite shocked to see how angry this idea seemed to make the Doctor. Surely he wasn't that naïve?

'You can't turn back time, Doctor. Progress is a one-way street.'

The Doctor shook his head vehemently. 'No, no, no. That's where you're wrong. It's cyclic. What goes up must come down. You can break the cycle, although it takes imagination and willpower and real effort. But if you don't, your empire will fall just like every other empire before it. You can't ignore history.'

'I don't,' said the professor, taking the ancient journal back from the Doctor and replacing it safely in its temperature-controlled container.

'Guillan's ship was the infamous SS *Armstrong*,' she went on, as if expecting him to recognise the name.

The Doctor looked blank and shrugged. 'Is that meant to mean something?'

'It was in the news for months,' she said, frowning.

'I travel a lot,' confessed the Doctor. 'I don't always get to catch up with current affairs.'

'Hardly current,' the professor replied. 'It was nearly fifty years ago!'

She explained that the SS *Armstrong* was notorious because of the mysterious circumstances in which it had been recovered. The ship had been found drifting, out of control and out of power, at the edge of Draconian space. An unknown disaster had befallen it and it had lost life support along with power. Whatever the reason, the entire crew had been killed.

'Any ideas what exactly happened to it?' asked the Doctor.

'Thousands,' the professor replied, 'each one more unlikely than the last. All we know for certain is that when an imperial cruiser patrolling the no-fly zone recovered it, the salvage team found they weren't the first to have gone on board since the accident. Space pirates had stripped the ship of everything of value.'

'But that's not the whole story, is it?' guessed the Doctor.

The professor smiled and shook her head. 'There were traces of trisilicate in the hold. Scans revealed that the ship had been carrying an enormous stock of the stuff.'

'Trisilicate,' mused the Doctor. 'A rare and valuable energy source...'

'The fuel my ship needs too,' agreed the professor.

'So, Guillan's exploration had been successful?'

'That's certainly what everyone thought. Although the ship had been stripped of most things, there were a few personal items left. Including a handful of images printed out and stuck on the wall of Guillan's cabin. They were various views of the same planet and had been labelled in his own hand. Two words described each image – Laylora and paradise.'

'Hence the legend of the "Paradise Planet"?'

The professor nodded. 'You know how myths develop. It's like a snowball. It starts with a kernel of truth and builds and builds until… well, it becomes something far greater. It takes on the status of legend. And that's what happened with Laylora. Soon that's all people were talking about. Everyone had a theory about where it could be found.'

The Doctor was taking all this in. 'A holy grail for a new generation…' he murmured.

'If you like. For a while it was all the rage – everyone and his electronic dog were looking for the legendary Paradise Planet. But when no one found it the interest faded. Something else came along to capture the public imagination and everyone forgot the name Laylora…'

'Except for you,' the Doctor guessed. 'What kept you looking when everyone else had given up?'

'I came across this journal. And when I read it, I knew it was the genuine article. It's a personal diary, not a log of his journey, but Guillan has described the places he visited along the way. With a lot of hard work, I've been able to plot his route. And that's what brought me here.'

'But why were you so sure it was genuine?' asked the Doctor.

The professor moved away, not meeting the Doctor's eyes. She's hiding something, he thought, but what?

'I just thought there had to be something in it,' she offered by way of an explanation eventually, but clearly there was more to it than she was willing to admit.

'Is it me or is it hot in here?' asked the Doctor, loosening his tie.

'What?' The professor was finding it difficult to keep up with the Doctor's kangaroo-like mind.

'I said it seems a bit on the warm side,' said the Doctor, feeling around the cabin wall with the palm of his hand.

'Now you come to mention it, it does feel a bit hotter than usual.'

The Doctor sniffed the air. 'It *is* getting warmer. Where are your environment controls?' A worried expression appeared on his face. 'I think you may have a problem.'

SIX

It was now fully dark outside the tent, but the light from the fire was enough for Rose to see what she was doing. The soup hadn't lasted long and an equally tasty plate of salad and vegetables had followed. While they enjoyed their meal, Rose had bombarded Rez with questions about his life on Laylora and the teenager, excited to have another human being to talk to, was happy to tell her everything she wanted to know.

The tribe lived in harmony with nature, Rez told her solemnly, which would have sounded really naff from most people, but sounded utterly sincere and reasonable when he said it. It seemed an idyllic lifestyle, although Rose was fairly certain it wouldn't appeal to her in the long term. Perhaps it was just all a bit too perfect, and she said as much to Rez. He laughed, amused at the comment.

'Perfect? I don't think it's perfect… it's just balanced. Everything plays its part. If something bad happens, something good will happen to keep the balance.'

Rose found herself nodding; that seemed to make sense. But then Rez's face darkened, as a breeze made the flames of the fire flicker and falter. 'At least, that's how it used to be…' There was a sadness in his voice that he couldn't disguise.

'What's changed?' asked Rose gently.

Rez shrugged. 'I'm not sure… No one is. But recently there have been more bad things than good. Some of the harvest failed last year. There have been tremors. Storms. Strange weather.'

All this sounded a bit familiar to Rose. 'You've not got a case of global warming, have you?'

The phrase meant little to Rez. 'I don't know about warming, but there is something wrong. And it seems to be getting worse.'

Rose felt sorry for him. It was clear that he loved this place and it was hurting him that things were going wrong. She wondered if the crashed spaceship had something to do with it. The Doctor would find out. Perhaps together they could work out what the problem was.

'So what's with Brother H and his mumbo-jumbo?' she asked, trying to change the subject.

This brought a smile back to Rez's face. 'He's harmless, you know.'

'Harmless? He wanted to sacrifice me to your planet!' exclaimed Rose.

'He's just like the rest of us, trying to make sense of a changing world.'

'So you lot don't make a habit of sacrifices and all that?'

Rez shook his head, still smiling. 'Not as a rule. At least not for hundreds of years. A long time ago our ancestors did. But we grew out of it.' Rez stopped and corrected himself. 'I should say "their ancestors", shouldn't I?'

Rose let the comment pass. 'So what's Brother Hugan, then – a throwback?'

Rez shrugged. 'He is the tribe's wise man, our shaman. He studies the old ways and tries to find the wisdom among the superstition.'

'And that costume you were wearing – what was that all about?'

'It's for use in certain ceremonies. It's meant to represent the Witiku.'

Rose remembered the name. 'The creatures the planet calls on to protect itself?'

Rez was impressed. 'That's right. You were paying attention!'

'I try.'

Rose smiled to herself. Take that, Mrs Cooper, she thought. *Rose Tyler would have reached a better standard in History this year if she had managed to listen as enthusiastically as she speaks.* That was one school report which had, mysteriously, never found its way home.

'The Witiku are meant to appear in times of great danger,' explained Rez. 'That's why Brother Hugan is so worried about the crop failures and the weird weather. He fears the Witiku will walk again. Maybe they already are. Maybe that's what happened to –' Rez suddenly stopped.

'What?' demanded Rose.

Rez shook his head. 'We're not meant to talk about it.'

'Talk about what?' insisted Rose. 'Come on. Maybe the Doctor and I can help.'

Rez looked into her eyes and could see that she was genuine. He took a deep breath and then told her.

'Yesterday, three people disappeared. Brother Aerack, Brother Purin and Sister Serenta. They were digging a new animal trap and they never came home. We searched and searched, but there's been no sign of them. They've just vanished.' He stopped and looked away. 'People are saying the Witiku took them.'

'I'm sorry,' said Rose.

'They're just kids, my age. And they've just gone, Rose. Completely gone!'

The Doctor hurried along the spaceship corridor, leaving Professor Shulough trailing in his wake.

'Next door on the right,' she called after him, rather out of breath.

She couldn't quite work out how it was that a man who had been their prisoner a few minutes ago was now acting as if he owned the place. Somehow he had persuaded her to accept him at face value. 'Trust me,' he had said, and she did.

The Doctor reached the door she'd indicated and stabbed at the controls without any success.

'Some power systems are still off-line,' she explained.

'So I can't use the sonic screwdriver,' muttered the Doctor, with a sigh. 'I'll just have to improvise, then.' He started searching about for something, anything, he could use instead. 'We'll have to open the door manually,' he explained, dropping to his knees and tugging at a flooring panel. With a grunt of satisfaction he pulled the floor tile free and flexed it between his hands. 'This might do the trick.'

He got to his feet and started trying to squeeze the floor tile between the frame and the door. Both had been edged with some kind of rubber padding to prevent noise and to limit wear and tear, so the flexible floor tile was able to make some headway.

Patiently the Doctor fed the tile through as much as he could, then he began to pull it away from the frame. The door began to move, only fractionally at first, but enough for the professor to slip her fingers into the gap. She began to pull and the Doctor joined her.

Now there was a clear gap of a couple of centimetres between the frame and the door. Together the Doctor and Professor Shulough forced the door open. From the room beyond came the sound of something burning and acrid smoke began to assault their nostrils. With a final joint effort the door sprang fully back and they could see into the room. Not that there was much to see. Clouds of noxious smoke poured out into the corridor. The Doctor clasped a handkerchief over his nose and mouth and pushed his way through the smoke into the room. The professor followed him as best she could.

'Something must have shorted,' she hazarded, seeing the environmental-control panels ablaze.

She looked around for the fire extinguisher but the cradle was empty. The reason soon became clear as the Doctor unleashed a jet of fire-killing chemical foam, which quickly did its job.

As the fire spluttered and died and the smoke cleared, they both became aware of a third figure in the room, lying prone on the floor to one side of the console that had caught alight. It was a crew member and he appeared to be dead.

The Doctor gave the body a quick examination, but he quickly realised that nothing could be done for the poor man.

'I'm sorry,' he said finally, and he meant it. In his long life he'd seen too much death and it always hurt.

'No need to apologise,' came the casual reply from the professor, who seemed more interested in picking apart the remains of the console. 'You put the fire out, didn't you?'

The Doctor's eyes narrowed. 'I was talking about your crew member. He's dead,' the Doctor told her coolly. Then he got to his feet and joined the professor, a dangerous look playing across his face. 'According to his uniform tag, his name is Collins.'

Perhaps feeling the intensity of the Doctor's gaze, the professor turned and looked over in the direction of the body. She nodded. 'Jae Collins. How sad.' But to the Doctor's ears, sadness was the last thing she was feeling. He'd met Cybermen with more sympathy than this woman. Either she had a real problem expressing emotion or she was a real monster. For the moment the Doctor was prepared to give her the benefit of the doubt.

'Still, he didn't have any vital duties. His loss shouldn't affect our mission.'

'Vital duties!' The Doctor was almost beside himself with fury. 'A man's just lost his life!'

The professor still looked unconcerned. 'He knew the risks. Deep-space travel is always dangerous.' And with that the professor turned back to examining the damage to the environmental controls.

The Doctor shook his head sadly, but before he could say anything else Kendle arrived. He shot a suspicious look at the Doctor and pulled out his hand weapon. 'Was this anything to do with you?'

'Hardly,' replied the Doctor, raising his hands as a precaution. 'I was still locked up when this started.'

'It was thanks to the Doctor that the fire was extinguished as quickly as it was and before it could spread any further,' explained the professor.

Kendle's brows furrowed but he nodded and lowered his weapon. 'In that case I guess I owe you an apology. And my thanks.'

'Anything to be of service,' said the Doctor lightly, and stepped smartly out of the way, allowing Kendle to see Collins's body for the first time.

If it was a test Kendle passed with flying colours.

'Collins! Is he… What – what happened?' The words tumbled out as the older man hurried over to see for himself. He looked at the professor and then at the Doctor for an explanation.

'Smoke inhalation,' said the Doctor simply. 'There was nothing anyone could have done.'

'But what was he doing in here?' asked Kendle.

'Judging from his position, I think he was trying to use the manual override to reset the sprinkler system,' the Doctor suggested, waving a hand in the direction of the ceiling, which, like most in the spaceship, was decorated with tiny emergency sprinkler taps. 'I guess the heat sensors are among the systems that are still off-line.'

Kendle nodded an acknowledgement. 'A lot of what we thought were non-essential systems were kept off-line after the crash, so we could run other computers.' He inclined his head in the direction of the professor but stopped short of actually blaming her directly. The moment was not lost on the Doctor, who made a mental note to find out later exactly how much the two disagreed about what was and what was not essential.

'We'll have to take his body home for burial. His family will want us to,' Kendle told the professor, getting to his feet.

THE PRICE OF PARADISE

The professor waved him away. 'Make whatever arrangements you need to make,' she told him, 'and send young Hespell up here to help me get this fixed.'

With a last, slightly embarrassed look in the direction of the Doctor, Kendle left.

'Perhaps I can help?' offered the Doctor. 'I don't like to blow my own trumpet, but I am exceedingly good at this techy stuff.' He was giving her the full charm offensive, but getting very little back in return.

Professor Shulough considered him for a long moment with her cold, dark eyes. 'How can I refuse an offer like that?' she said finally, and stepped aside to let the Doctor get at the blackened panel.

They seemed to have been talking for hours. When Rose poked her head outside the tent she saw that most of the other fires had already been extinguished. The rest of the tribe must have gone to sleep ages ago. She realised that it had been a long time since she'd done anything as normal as this. Just spending a few hours with someone she'd just met had been really fun. Not crazy fun, like being with the Doctor, but a normal kind of fun, down to earth, more like spending an evening with Mickey, eating chips and putting the world to rights.

The thought of Mickey made Rose aware of what it was she was finding so attractive in Rez. It was his Mickeyness: his youthful energy and relentless cheerfulness.

Rez was back at the fire, mixing up a hot drink in another pot.

'What happens now?' asked Rose a little shyly.

'Now? Now we have a nice cup of jinnera,' replied Rez with a broad smile.

Rose had no idea what jinnera was, but she hoped it was something not too different from tea. It was one of the few things that her mother and the Doctor had in common – they did both like a good cup of tea. And so did Rose. Trouble was, on board the TARDIS the Doctor had such a collection of exotic teas that Rose never got to have a good old-fashioned normal cuppa. Was it too much to hope that this jinnera tasted like PG Tips?

Apparently it was. Jinnera turned out to be more of a coffee-style drink, but with a hint of chocolate to it. It was, Rose had to admit, rather tasty. So much so that she quickly drained the cup she had been given.

'Any chance of another?' she asked cheekily.

Rez went to make her a fresh cup. 'Two is the limit, though. You can have too much of a good thing.'

Rose pulled a face. 'Not when something is as good as this!' she insisted.

Rez shook his head firmly. 'In this case, no. Overdose on the jinnen bean and you'll sleep for ever. It makes you feel good, but too much relaxes you so much that your heart just stops.'

Rose hesitated, her hand in mid-air, about to take back her refilled cup.

'Don't worry,' Rez assured her. 'Two won't kill you.'

After only a slight pause, she accepted the proffered drink.

'So, you think Brother Hugan's on to something, then, do you? With all his talk of the old ways…'

'I don't know. I'm sure the ancients weren't fools, though. You've seen the remains of their temple.'

Rose frowned and realised what it was that had been bugging her. 'How come you live in these tents and not buildings?'

'People change. We live nomadic lives now, closer to nature. No one's lived in buildings for hundreds of years.'

'Maybe they were scared off by those Witiku,' joked Rose, but disappointingly Rez didn't laugh.

Instead he took her comment at face value. 'Perhaps they were,' he admitted.

Rose was surprised. 'You think there really was some kind of creature like that suit you were wearing?'

Rez looked her straight in the eyes. 'Yes, I do. I've seen too much at the temple and around it. Murals, paintings, statues. I'm sure the Witiku were real once.'

Seeing Rose's face, Rez hurriedly reassured her. 'But that was all a long time ago. I don't think we're going to be seeing a Witiku any time soon,' he promised her.

And at that precise moment, a fist of razor-sharp talons ripped through the wall of the tent, missing Rose by centimetres.

SEVEN

Rose jumped to her feet and dived forward. Behind her the savage talons sliced again and again through the fabric of the tent. But there was a more unpleasant sound as well, an animalistic grunting and roaring, plus, from slightly further away, more ripping and screaming. Where, a moment ago, there had been a solid wall of leather there was now a mass of thin shreds, like the plastic strips her nan used to have on her back door in the summer. Stepping through this new entrance was a creature that Rose recognised instantly as a Witiku.

The costume that Rez had been wearing earlier didn't do justice to the real thing. For a start it was huge. It was similar to a werewolf, but Rose knew this was no wolf. It had a distinct smell, a strong animal odour of sweat and zoos. The creature was covered with a dense coat of coarse dark hair, which made it hard to see in the dark. For a moment time seemed to stand still. Rose realised with a shudder of fear that there were actually four sets of talons as the terrifying creature had two extra arms. The head, thrown back as it roared angrily, was an ugly mass of hair and fangs, with wild red eyes that showed no sign of intelligence. This was pure animal, wild and majestic. Around its neck something shiny and glittery caught the light, but Rose couldn't make out what it was.

As luck would have it, she'd jumped the wrong way. Another Witiku had now appeared, cutting off her path to the main exit of the tent. Rose tried to stay calm, knowing that fear and panic would only put her in more danger. She looked around, desperately, for something – anything – she could use as a weapon. Her eyes alighted on the steaming-hot cup of jinnera. Shame to waste a good cuppa, she thought, but needs must. She grabbed the cup and threw the contents in the direction of the nearest creature's face.

To her surprise, it squealed and retreated, clearly in pain. Rose was amazed. Surely the jinnera hadn't been that hot? But whatever the reason for its success, her makeshift weapon was certainly having a devastating effect. The creature fell to its knees and was clutching at its face with two of its hands, while the other two waved wildly. The talons were retractable, Rose noted, and the creature seemed to be trying to scrape every drop of jinnera off its coat with its three-fingered hands.

'Rose, quick!'

It was Rez, at the tent flap, beckoning to her. Taking care to keep clear of the floundering lower arms, which still had the talons fully exposed, Rose ducked around the creature she had brought to its knees and joined Rez. The blond boy grabbed her hand – so like the Doctor, thought Rose again – and pulled her out into the night.

The village was in pandemonium. People were screaming and panicking, running in all directions. One or two of them had burning torches, but most of the Laylorans were, quite literally, in the dark. It was impossible to see how many of the creatures were attacking them.

The one that Rose had thrown her drink at staggered out of Rez's tent, all but bringing it down around him. Rez urged Rose to follow him.

At the edge of the village they found Brother Hugan, shouting and gesticulating. At first Rose thought the witch doctor had lost his mind, but then she realised that he was actually trying to herd the frightened villagers away from danger.

'We need to get to the temple,' he was calling. 'Don't panic, just hurry…'

Rez and Rose tried to help. A small child had managed to lose her mother and sister and was sitting by an extinguished fire, crying and obviously terrified. Rose picked her up and carried her towards the line of people now disappearing into the dark forest, in the direction of the temple. Rez recognised the child and helped Rose find her mother.

Rose felt an odd shudder of empathy when she saw

the look on the Layloran mother's face as she was reunited with her little girl. It was the look she saw on her mum's face every time the Doctor took her home to the Powell Estate for a visit.

The screams were less frequent now and there was no immediate sign of the attackers. Further back in the darkness of the village they could still be heard, though, crashing through the tents as if looking for victims.

'What do they want?' Rose asked out loud.

'I didn't fancy stopping to ask them,' confessed Rez.

Somewhere out in the forest they could hear Brother Hugan urging the refugees on towards safety. Rez and Rose seemed to be the last people left at the village's edge. Rose looked back, as one of the creatures appeared, with an unconscious villager on his shoulder.

'They're taking people!' she cried.

'If you don't come now, you'll be next.' Rez insisted, and Rose allowed him to lead her away.

The forest was much less idyllic at night, Rose discovered. A pair of glowing moons in the star-speckled sky gave some light, but it was all filtered through the canopy of trees, making life at ground level rather murky. The floor of the forest was treacherous, what with creepers and tree roots, and more than once Rose fell and had to be helped up by the nimble-footed Rez. She was surprised how at home the human boy seemed to be here, making his way through with the ease that Rose had when navigating Oxford Street on a shopping trip. He seemed to be able to sense obstructions, leaping over fallen trees before she had even registered them. So, she thought with a grin, not only Superman but Tarzan as well!

Behind them she thought she could hear sounds of pursuit, but after a while these faded and she was pretty sure they were no longer being followed.

Short of breath, she stopped, bent over and placed her hands on her knees. Rez, ahead of her as always, skidded to a stop and doubled back to join her.

'Are you all right?' he asked.

'I just need a minute,' she gasped.

Rose seemed to do a lot of running in her adventures with the Doctor but somehow it was never enough for her to get used to doing this sort of thing effortlessly.

Suddenly Rez pulled her to the ground, rolling her into the cover of a large bush.

'Oi!' she began. 'You can cut that out!'

But he covered her mouth with his palm and hissed a 'Sssh' into her ear. Something was moving nearby.

Rose gulped and nodded at Rez to indicate that it was safe to remove his hand. She wasn't going to make a noise. At least not consciously. But she was all too aware of her heart thumping in her chest, surely loud enough to be heard above the sounds of the forest. The footsteps came nearer.

Rose squeezed her eyes shut and tried to shrink

inside herself. Just go past, she thought, just go past. Suddenly the bush she was hiding under was pulled aside and something reached down towards her.

It was Mother Jaelette.

'You nearly scared me half to death,' she whispered at her angrily, but the Layloran woman didn't seem particularly concerned about that.

'Quick. Come with me,' she whispered back, dragging Rose out from her cover and forcing Rez to follow.

She began to lead them through the forest. Rose caught glimpses of the temple buildings to her left and realised that they were walking around it.

'Did everyone get away?' Rez asked.

Mother Jaelette nodded. 'Those that escaped are fine. But there are still some people unaccounted for…'

'And what about the creatures?' asked Rose.

Mother Jaelette turned to her and put a finger to her lips. 'That's what I want to show you,' she whispered. 'Look…'

She pulled back a curtain of vines and Rose and Rez were able to see them shuffling away in the distance. For a moment it looked like a school outing, with the creatures walking along in crocodile fashion, but then the moonlight caught the vicious claws and Rose remembered how deadly and dangerous they were.

'Where are they going?' she asked, but even as she spoke she had an idea of the answer. 'That's the direction of the crashed spaceship, isn't it?'

Rez nodded. 'I think so.'

Rose thought for a moment about what this meant. Were the creatures connected to the spaceship somehow? But the Doctor had been taken away by men, not monsters. She was missing something, some connection. If only the Doctor were here.

'I have to get to that ship in the morning,' she announced.

'But that's where the creatures are going…' Rez pointed out.

'Which is why I have to go there,' Rose replied determinedly.

Rez could see that she wouldn't change her mind. 'Very well,' he said. 'I'll take you at Saxik rise.'

The last of the beasts had disappeared now. Mother Jaclette started to lead them back to the parts of the temple site that the tribe were using as a haven.

'Did you notice something odd about the Witiku?' she asked them as they walked carefully through the dark forest.

'Odd?' retorted Rose. 'They're two-metre-high hairy monsters with claws the size of skewers, how odd do they have to be?'

'How many Witiku attacked the village tonight?' asked Jaelette, ignoring her sarcasm.

Rose wasn't sure she could answer that.

'A handful… Three or four,' she estimated.

Rez had a much clearer idea. 'There were three. The two that attacked us and one other.'

Mother Jaelette stopped and turned to look at them. The moonlight hit her face and Rose could see the strain of what had happened etched there.

'Exactly,' she said in a weary tone.

With a sudden rush of understanding Rose caught on to what she was getting at. 'But just now… we saw a dozen of them or more, heading for the spaceship.'

Mother Jaelette looked grim. 'Brother Hugan was right. The Witiku army is growing. Another night like tonight and they will outnumber us.'

Rose thought she had the answer.

'If Brother Hugan knows so much about the things, maybe he knows a way to stop them.'

Jaelette shook her head sadly.

'You're right that he knows more about the Witiku than any of us,' Jaelette told her solemnly, 'but Brother Hugan is one of the missing!'

Trainee Pilot Jonn Hespell had been amused when the Doctor persuaded Professor Shulough that she'd stumbled across quite an asset in capturing him. The environmental-control system had been a piece of cake for the stranger to fix, and having sorted that out he'd been foolish enough to volunteer his services for any other little jobs she might have. Three hours later Hespell suspected that the Doctor was beginning to wonder if this might have been a mistake. Having just survived a crash landing, there were dozens of 'little jobs' that needed his attention, and Hespell had been assigned the task of shepherding their new super-mechanic from problem to problem.

'The thing is,' announced the Doctor, as he followed Hespell through the narrow crawl-spaces of the engineering deck, 'it's not a matter of what's damaged, it's more of question of trying to identify something that isn't!'

'It wasn't that bad a landing,' Hespell said loyally.

'Oh no, any landing you can walk away from and all that,' commented the Doctor, his eyes twinkling. 'Was it you at the controls, then?'

Hespell blushed and shook his head.

'Major Kendle,' he confessed.

'Ah,' exclaimed the Doctor, 'older-driver syndrome. I understand. Of course, by that reckoning I'm too old to drive anything more than a motorised zimmer frame, so maybe I shouldn't be too critical.'

Hespell couldn't make head or tail of anything the Doctor said. Was he really trying to claim that he was older than Kendle? He looked again at the Doctor, but there was no sign of any cosmetic work. He really did look to be in his thirties.

Meanwhile, the Doctor stole a glance at his guide, amused to see the confusion on his face. That was good. Confused people were more likely to tell you the things you needed to know. In his experience – which was, in this field, pretty considerable – keeping people off balance was a useful tactic.

'So, tell me about this ship. Bit of a mongrel, isn't it?'

Wrong-footed again by the sudden change of subject, Hespell couldn't find a way to evade the question. Which was exactly what the Doctor wanted.

'I guess so. It started out as a pleasure vehicle, I think. But it's had a few upgrades over the years.'

'And how long have you been part of the crew?'

Hespell shrugged. Sometimes it was easy to lose track of time completely on a job like this. 'About eighteen months,' he answered, 'give or take.'

The Doctor nodded as if this was the most interesting thing he'd ever heard. 'Privately funded? That's rare these days, isn't it?'

'That's why I signed up,' Hespell confessed. 'Who wants a boring life in one of the corporate fleets? Professor Shulough was offering a good old-fashioned adventure.'

'And did you get it?'

The Doctor was examining the engine cradles. Old-fashioned dark-rimmed spectacles had appeared from somewhere and he was peering at the read-out screens carefully.

'What?' asked Hespell, confused again.

'The adventure she promised. Did you get it?'

Hespell thought about this for a moment and then shook his head. 'Not a lot. Most of the time it's been very, very tedious. Until today of course.' Hespell laughed, a tad embarrassed. 'Now I'm getting more adventure than I bargained for!'

The Doctor was using some kind of tool to seal a

loose connection. The device buzzed and glowed with a strange blue light. 'There. That should do it,' he announced triumphantly. 'That should start recharging now. Give it twenty-four hours or so and you might just be able to think about trying to fly this thing again.' He looked around, puzzled. 'If the trisilicate engines are off-line where's your power coming from?'

'Emergency generator,' Hespell said, as if it was obvious.

The Doctor's eyes narrowed, almost imperceptibly. 'Show me.'

The young crewman led the stranger back through the engines and up to the main deck of the craft. 'We set it up in the cargo bay,' he explained, as they reached a pair of double doors.

'Really?' The Doctor sounded suspicious. 'Why's that, then?'

Hespell activated the door controls and the answer became obvious. At the rear of the room was an ugly-looking metal machine which was giving off a terrible stench.

'It's a bit… antisocial,' apologised Hespell.

'Antisocial? That's an understatement!' Despite the foul smell the Doctor approached the machine to look at it more closely. 'Is this really what I think it is?'

'It's a micro-fusion generator,' Hespell admitted.

The Doctor looked seriously unhappy. 'Technology that is banned on most civilised planets. What on earth is this monstrosity doing here?'

Hespell looked a little embarrassed. 'It was the smallest but most effective back-up power source. Apparently.'

'Smallest and dirtiest,' the Doctor retorted, glaring at it with an intensity that would have made most people want to shrivel up and die on the spot. 'Where are the coolant filters?'

'There, er, aren't any.' Hespell couldn't even look him in the eye now.

'So where are you venting the –'

The Doctor broke off as he spotted the answer to his own question. From the rear of the machine a pair of clear hoses were carrying dirty yellow liquid away. The hoses led to a hatch in the wall of the room. The Doctor ran over to examine it.

'Tell me this leads to some kind of safe waste-disposal system,' he demanded sternly, fearing the worst.

Hespell shook his head, keeping his eyes directed at the floor.

'It just goes outside,' he said in a quiet voice.

The Doctor got to his feet and moved swiftly to the door. 'I need to speak to Professor Shulough,' he announced, and disappeared before Hespell could stop him.

The professor and Kendle were in the lab, looking over the latest scan results, when the door burst open and the Doctor spilled into the room, like a force of nature.

'Come in,' said the professor sarcastically.

'You have to shut down that generator,' the Doctor said in a voice that suggested any argument would be a waste of time.

'I'm sorry?'

'You're pouring toxic waste on to this planet's surface, in violation of every rule in the book. You have to shut it down.' The Doctor's eyes burned with passion. He couldn't believe how stupid and irresponsible these humans were being.

'We're a long way from the Empire's courts, Doctor. This far from home, we have to make our own rules.'

'I thought you were looking for paradise? Do you want to destroy it before you've had a chance to look around?'

Professor Shulough just shook her head. 'Don't be so melodramatic, Doctor. It's a big planet. Even if we run the generator for a week, it's only a drop in the ocean.'

The Doctor looked aghast. 'How dare you? You're visitors here. Can't you treat the planet with some respect?'

The professor crossed her arms and leaned back on her console, preparing herself for a long argument, but she never got her chance as Hespell came running into the room.

Kendle sighed. 'Doesn't anyone knock any more?'

'Sorry, sir,' gasped Hespell, 'but they're back. The creatures. And this time there are more of them!'

* * *

On the bridge the repairs had progressed well and the full complement of hull cameras were now operational again. And the view screen showed that Hespell was right – at least a dozen of the creatures were emerging from the inky black of the forest. The cameras switched to infrared and they could see them in more detail as they swarmed towards the ship.

'Break out the small arms,' Kendle ordered, and led the way to the armoury, which was a large cupboard at the rear of the bridge.

When unlocked, this proved to be stuffed to the gills with various kinds of handguns and other weapons. The Doctor recognised the stun blaster that Hespell had used on him earlier.

'Stun settings only,' he suggested, not wishing to be part of a massacre.

'Do those talons of theirs have a stun setting?' retorted Kendle sarcastically.

The Doctor stepped up to the man and eyeballed him. 'And how many times have they used those talons on one of you? They've not hurt you at all. It's not you they're concerned with.'

For a moment the Doctor thought he was getting the message through, but Kendle roughly pushed him aside. 'Come on,' he ordered the rest of the crew. 'With me. At the double.'

He headed out, followed by Hespell and Baker.

Professor Shulough picked up the stun blaster. 'Make yourself useful,' she suggested, indicating that the Doctor should help himself to a weapon.

'No, thanks,' he said hurriedly. 'I'm allergic to the things.'

'I wouldn't have taken you for a coward,' replied the professor.

'And I wouldn't have taken you for a fool. It's not cowardice,' said the Doctor in a steely tone. 'I just don't like guns. They stop people thinking.'

The professor simply glared at him. 'Then don't get in our way.'

When the Doctor caught up with the crew they had fanned out from the airlock doors and found cover as best they could in the clearing. So far they were having some success in holding back the creatures, but despite the superiority of their firepower they were clearly outnumbered.

Kendle, leading from the front, was the furthest away from the spaceship, while Hespell and Baker had found positions at either side of the airlock. Professor Shulough was looking out from the edge of the doorway.

'It's too dark out there,' she complained.

The Doctor's eyes had already adjusted to the lack of light. 'This isn't a random attack, you realise. They want something.'

'Yes. Us.'

The Doctor shook his head. 'Something else.' There was a noise from above, a metallic clanging. 'They're on the hull!' he exclaimed, but it was too late.

Two of the creatures dropped down from above, directly in front of them. The professor raised her weapon, but the Doctor pulled her back before she could use it. He pinned both her arms to her side. 'Let them in. Find out what they want.'

The woman struggled in his grip. 'Let go of me, you idiot. They'll kill us.'

'No, I don't think so,' the Doctor insisted, and, as if to prove him right, the two giants moved straight past the pair of them and disappeared into the ship.

The Doctor let go of the professor, who was looking open-mouthed in the direction the creatures had taken. The Doctor called out into the dark, 'Hold your fire. Let them pass!'

When he turned back, he found that the professor had already set off after the invaders. The Doctor was torn between helping the crew outside and chasing after her. A moment later he was running back down the ship's corridors. He had a good idea where they would be going and headed directly for the cargo bay. He quickly caught up with the professor, who was waiting outside the double doors.

'They're in there,' she told him.

'I thought they might be,' he said, trying not to sound smug. 'I think you've just been invaded by radical environmentalists.'

Awful crashing sounds of destruction could be heard from within.

'They're smashing the generator...' The Professor couldn't believe it.

'I told you,' the Doctor reminded her. 'It was polluting the planet.'

Suddenly the lights in the corridor went out. The power was off again. The double doors were pulled open by force and the two creatures came lumbering out. Behind them the generator had been completely taken apart. The creatures ignored the Doctor and the professor and headed back towards the airlock.

They followed the monsters at a discreet distance. Outside they found the gunfire had died down. The battle seemed to be over for now, but it hadn't been without casualties. Kendle was attending to the female crew member, Baker, who had a nasty-looking wound across her shoulder.

Hespell was peering out into the darkness. 'They just suddenly went,' he told the professor.

The Doctor nodded. 'They found what they came for.'

'Let's get inside and secure the ship,' ordered Professor Shulough, without giving the injured woman a second look.

The Doctor watched the professor with cool eyes. She didn't seem to feel anything. Could she really be that heartless, or was this lack of empathy a mask she wore?

'Here, let me help,' he said, bending to look at Baker's wound.

'You're a medical doctor, then?' asked Kendle, interested.

'I'm a doctor of many things,' the Doctor told him without a trace of arrogance. 'Did the creatures suffer any casualties?' he asked as he gently picked up the now unconscious Baker and started walking back towards the ship.

'Just the one,' answered Kendle. 'Stunned, not dead.'

The Doctor met his eyes – perhaps his request to temper the level of violence had been heeded after all. 'We'd better bring him inside too,' suggested the Doctor. 'Put him somewhere secure, of course,' he added, seeing the alarm in Kendle's face. 'Just to be on the safe side.'

Kendle and Hespell went off into the darkness and reappeared a moment or two later with the heavy bulk of the unconscious monster between them. Even in this condition, it was still terrifying.

EIGHT

After all the excitement, Rose found it easier to sleep than she would have expected. As soon as she put her head down, on the rolled-up blanket Rez had given her to use as a pillow, she was asleep. It seemed like only moments later that she was stretching and opening her eyes again, but she felt so refreshed it was as if she'd been asleep for hours.

It took her a moment to get her bearings. She was always the same in a strange bed; she'd wake up thinking she was at home, expecting her mum to knock on the door any moment with a nice cup of tea. In all the travelling she had done with the Doctor, she'd had to grab sleep in quite a few odd places, but she still hadn't got any better at the waking-up bit. Some people are morning people and some people aren't, that's what her mum always said, and Rose just wasn't a morning person.

Of course, the Doctor was something else again. Rose had seen him apparently snatching the odd nap, but she wasn't convinced he ever actually went to bed.

This morning, however, Rose came to her senses remarkably quickly and felt alert straight away. Perhaps it was the adrenalin still running high in her blood after the events of the previous night. She was in a makeshift dormitory in one of the smaller buildings near the main temple. A couple of dozen Laylorans lay sleeping round her, a number of whom were gently snoring. Taking care not to make too much noise, she got to her feet and made her way to the door.

In the next room, a couple of jugs of water and some cups had been left out and there was a small fire over which a pot was bubbling with a now familiar smell. Jinnera. OK, thought Rose. While her preference would have been tea, or even coffee at a push, beggars couldn't be choosers. She helped herself to a cup of the brew and felt much better for it. Hadn't Rez said it was a feel-good drink? Rose decided he'd undersold it. A great pick-me-up and a weapon to use against monsters to boot!

Thinking back to her close encounter, it had been odd the way the creature had reacted to the drink, but Rose was sure she hadn't imagined it. They must be allergic to the stuff, she decided. One-nil to her!

Feeling even more alert now, Rose set about exploring her surroundings. It was dawn and, in stark contrast to the horrors of the previous night, the forest looked as peaceful and beautiful as it had when she and the Doctor had first arrived.

The sun was shining and birdsong filled the air. Rose couldn't help but smile; it was impossible not to. Despite everything that had happened, she felt good. She looked for Rez among the sleepers but, when she failed to find him, she decided to take the opportunity to explore the site alone.

Walking around the ruins of the ancient Layloran temple complex, Rose realised that it was more extensive than she and the Doctor had originally thought. The outer buildings had mostly fallen into ruin and the forest had crept back around them over the years. Between the trees what seemed to be moss-covered ridges were actually bits of walls. In time, no doubt the rest of the site would go the same way. She remembered her recent visit to ancient Rome and how odd it had been to see whole buildings that in her own time were just piles of old stone. All a matter of perspective, she concluded.

Rose found herself heading back towards the main temple, keen to see inside it. The heavy wooden door, decorated with intricate carvings, wasn't easy to shift, but she planted her feet and put her back into it and, eventually, the door moved. She stepped in without even bothering to try and close the door behind her.

No one could have doubted the purpose of the building. It was like every church she had ever been in – a large cavernous place, full of religious iconography and with an atmosphere that somehow demanded reverence and filled the observer with a sense of peace.

Rose moved forward with careful steps, not wanting to make any unnecessary noise. Around the walls were a number of massive statues, many of a woman, presumably the human form of the planet herself. Other statues were of more familiar creatures – the Witiku, as she now knew them. Above the figures were galleries – like boxes at a theatre – that would have allowed the ancient Laylorans a bird's-eye view of the ceremonies. And at the end of the room there was a stone slab that could only have been an altar. She noted with some disgust that the stone was marked with a number of dark stains. She swallowed hard and moved on. In an alcove to one side she found some steps leading down to a lower level. Grabbing a flaming torch from a wall bracket, Rose began the descent.

When Hespell woke, the first thing he did, after washing and dressing, was to go to the MedLab to check on Ania Baker. He found her lying in her bed, looking pale but a good deal happier than when he'd last seen her. The medical scanners were humming quietly, indicating that all was well. With the 'dirty' back-up generator out of commission, they were relying on the ship's nearly empty emergency batteries, but the Doctor had constructed a device from odds and ends that was functioning as a regulator, helping to eke out the remaining power. Professor Shulough was confident that they would find the trisilicate they needed for the main engines before they ran out of power completely.

'How are you this morning?' Hespell asked, sitting gingerly on the side of Baker's bed.

'It hurts,' she confessed, 'but thanks to you I think I'm going to be OK.'

'Me?' Hespell blushed.

'You stunned the creature that got me. If you hadn't acted when you did, his next blow would have disembowelled me. So thanks.'

Hespell tried to look nonchalant. 'I'd have done the same for anyone,' he told her.

Ania reached out a hand and touched his arm. 'But you did it for me. And that's what counts.'

She smiled at him with a new warmth and he felt himself turning an even deeper shade of red.

'Is it me or is it hot in here?' he muttered, pulling at his uniform around the neckline.

Baker shook her head gently. 'I don't think so.' She grinned, amused at his discomfort. It was rather endearing, she thought.

'Must just be me, then,' muttered Hespell, getting to his feet.

He felt an urgent need to change the subject. Looking around the MedLab, he realised that the Doctor wasn't around. His brown coat was slung over the back of a chair, but other than that there was no sign of him.

'Where is the Doctor?' he asked Baker.

'With his other patient,' Ania told him.

Hespell looked a bit confused.

Baker fixed him with a sharp look. 'It wasn't just us out there, was it?'

Hespell found the Doctor and the 'other patient' in the cargo bay, which had been adjudged the best place to act as a holding cell. Hespell had refused the suggestion of using his cabin again but it had never really been a possibility; this new prisoner was rather larger than the Doctor.

The Doctor looked up as he heard the doors open and was pleased to see that it was the young trainee pilot. Both the professor and Kendle were hopelessly fixed in their worldviews but Hespell showed signs of having some imagination, and he approved of that. He nodded a greeting at Hespell and returned to examining the unconscious creature.

'Is there any possibility of getting these off?' he asked, gesturing at the heavy metal chains that were wrapped around the creature, which lay sprawled on its back in the middle of the floor.

Hespell looked at the chains, which were fixed to points on the walls that had originally been intended to support shelving units. They were stretched tight, pinning the creature securely to the floor. It looked, and probably was, painful.

'I'm sorry Doctor, but the professor says this thing

has to be restrained.' He could see the sadness in the Doctor's eyes and felt guilty, but he dared not disobey a direct order.

'I don't think he's dangerous,' explained the Doctor, 'I really don't.'

'Tell that to Baker,' muttered Hespell.

'Baker went out there and started shooting at them. You all did. They only wanted to stop you from poisoning the planet. Once this –' the Doctor waved an arm in the general direction of the wrecked generator – 'this obscenity was destroyed they just left, didn't they?'

Hespell had to admit that the Doctor had a point.

'What are they?' he wondered.

The Doctor shrugged. 'I don't know. But there's more to them than meets the eye, I'm sure of that.'

Hespell came closer, intrigued. Even asleep, the creature looked fearsome. 'What do you mean?' he asked, bending and reaching out a curious hand to touch the alien fur.

'Well, they attacked as a group. There wasn't much sign of individuality, was there?' The Doctor looked to Hespell for confirmation.

'I – er, I suppose you're right,' he replied, not having thought about it much.

The Doctor continued with his theory. 'So that would suggest some kind of an animal that wasn't highly developed.'

Hespell nodded again.

'And yet,' said the Doctor, 'they knew exactly what they needed to do, which demonstrates a certain degree of intelligence.'

Hespell began to see what the Doctor was driving at. 'You mean they displayed characteristics of simple animals and more complex life forms at the same time?' he said.

To his delight, the Doctor broke into a broad smile. 'Good lad! You're using your brain!'

The Doctor gave him an encouraging pat on the shoulder, which threatened to knock him off balance and send him tumbling into the creature. The Doctor then reached over to pick at something on the monster's chest.

'So, now you've warmed up your noggin, what do you make of this?'

Hespell studied what the Doctor was holding. It was a necklace, decorated with colourful stones and crystals, threaded on to some kind of vine. The centrepiece was one enormous fist-sized yellow crystal. He gasped. 'Is that trisilicate?'

'Looks like it, doesn't it?' the Doctor agreed.

'Wow!'

'Which raises some rather interesting questions,' the Doctor announced, getting to his feet. 'For a start, when was the last time you saw a great big hairy monster like this wearing bling quite like that?'

The atmosphere in the temple crypt was chilly and

Rose shivered. She had discovered that it was far more than a simple room. Just as Rez had told her earlier, there was an absolute warren of interconnected cellars and tunnels down here that seemed to go on for kilometres. It was dark, cold and creepy, but fascinating at the same time. Rose found other images on the walls. They were fairly crude but clearly represented a range of ancient Layloran activities. They were even sketchier than the carvings the Doctor had been so fascinated by, the ones that decorated the exterior of the temple. In fact, now she thought about it, some of these tunnels and chambers seemed much older than the building above, as if perhaps the great temple had been built on top of an earlier, more primitive sacred place.

A repeated image depicted the Witiku. However, there was more to this underground area than just wall paintings. There were stores of grain and jinnen beans, and other materials too. Rose looked into one room and gasped in surprise. It was filled with a huge pile of crystals. Except, on closer examination, she found that what she had taken to be crystals were some kind of hard jewel, like yellow diamonds. And there were thousands of them. She picked one up to examine it more closely.

'Pretty, aren't they?'

Rose nearly jumped out of her skin. She whirled around to see who had crept up on her, but she already had an idea from the voice.

'Sister Kaylen!' The not-girlfriend. Terrific.

Rose had been aware of the girl shooting her dark looks 'all evening. She was clearly very fond of her stepbrother and Rose had half-expected her to join them for their 'date', but she'd stayed away. Rose stood up, dropping the jewel she'd just picked up. Although she had done nothing wrong, she still felt guilty.

'I wasn't going to take it!' she insisted, getting in her defence first.

Kaylen just shrugged. 'Take as many as you like. They're everywhere.'

Rose couldn't quite believe her ears. 'You don't value these things?'

She picked one up and felt its weight. It would make a lovely necklace, she thought.

The Layloran looked bemused. 'Value? What do you mean? They're pretty and we use them in our jewellery,' she continued, 'but they're ever so common. In the fields we find them all the time. It's a pain.'

A pain! Rose had to stop herself from laughing. Fields full of free jewellery and they think it's a problem!

'Were you looking for me?' Rose asked, wondering what she was doing there.

Kaylen nodded. 'I'm doing a head count,' she explained.

Suddenly the seriousness of what had happened last night came flooding back to Rose. She let Kaylen lead her back towards the staircase going up to the surface, all thoughts of the crystals forgotten.

'Are there many people missing?' she asked.

Kaylen nodded, a grim expression on her face. 'Eight, we think.'

Eight! The raid had been more successful than Rose had thought.

'Any sign of Brother Hugan?'

Kaylen shook her head sadly. 'No.'

Back on the surface, Rose and Kaylen found most of the adults gathered in an informal crisis meeting, discussing their options. As she had feared, an all-out attack on the spaceship was a popular choice, but not all the Laylorans were in favour. Mother Jaelette, for example, wanted to wait rather than rush into some foolish action that might just lead to more loss of life and she made her point forcibly.

Rose could see that both sides of the argument had their supporters, but neither commanded a majority. The one thing they all agreed on, though, was that what had happened was connected in some way with the crashed sky boat. She cleared her throat and tried to interrupt the debate, which was beginning to get a little heated.

'Excuse me,' she began, but her voice was drowned out. She tried again. 'Oi!' she cried, much louder, and this time she got their attention.

'Look, it's no good just shouting at each other.'

'You're an outsider – what do you know about this?' retorted one of the more belligerent elders.

Rose bristled but kept her cool. Losing her temper wouldn't help the situation at all.

'The people in that ship are human, like me. Like Rez here.'

Rez shot her an unhappy look, not pleased to be singled out like this.

'Perhaps I can talk to them, find out what they know. They may be able to help find your missing people.'

Mother Jaelette looked at her with interest. 'Is that likely?'

Rose nodded. 'They'll have technology, tools that might help…' And the Doctor's there, she thought to herself, he's worth a whole pile of tech all by himself.

To her relief she saw that Mother Jaelette was nodding; it looked like Rose had persuaded them not to take any action until this option had been explored. Rez stepped forward.

'I'll take you,' he said simply. 'I promised I would.'

'Thanks.' Rose smiled at him.

As Mother Jaelette gave him a big hug and told him to take care, Rose felt a twinge of guilt. She was taking Rez away from his family and she had an ominous feeling that he might never come back to them.

NINE

The walk through the forest was different this time. It was still as beautiful as ever and everywhere Rose looked there was another stunning vista to marvel at, but since the attack last night something subtle had changed for her. It might be a paradise but now she was very much aware that there could be monsters lurking all around.

Rez led the way, confidently striding through the maze of different trees, following the path the monsters had taken last night. They walked in silence, each occupied with their own thoughts.

Finally they reached an area where there were signs of damage to the tree tops.

'This must be where the ship came down,' Rez told her, pointing up at the broken branches.

A little further on they reached a clearing and there, battered but intact, was the spaceship.

Rose was getting a bit blasé about spaceships these days, but she'd never seen one quite like this. She could tell instantly that this was not a new ship. It looked a bit like one of the cars she used to see boys working on back home on the estate. Not new by any means, but well loved and showing signs of a long life of repairs. On the Powell Estate you'd see cars with bonnets and doors in colours that didn't match the rest of the car, and it was the same with this space vehicle. Panels looked to have been replaced by spares from entirely different ships, or possibly bits salvaged from junkyards.

'Perhaps that's why it crashed!' she speculated out loud.

Rez gave her a look. To him it was an amazing, technologically advanced machine and it was clearly intimidating him.

'Do you think it's safe to just walk up to it?' he asked.

Rose wasn't sure. 'We could go under a white flag?' she suggested.

Unfortunately a quick search of her pockets failed to produce anything that even faintly resembled a white flag, although Rose did find a half-empty packet of Polos, which was a bonus.

'Come on, then,' she said finally, popping a mint into her mouth and offering Rez one. 'Let's just walk slowly, keep our hands where they can see them and hope they don't fancy any target practice.'

A little nervously they stepped out of the cover offered by the trees and began to walk towards the spaceship. As they got closer Rose could see that the main airlock doors were open and there were a couple of people standing just inside.

'We come in peace,' she called out hopefully, adding, 'Don't shoot!'

'Rose Tyler, where the heck have you been?' called a familiar voice.

To Rose's shame she completely lost it. 'Doctor!'

She ran towards him and was delighted to see that he was running to meet her too. They collided in a giant bear hug that was probably *so* not cool, but Rose just didn't care. Sometimes being cool was just overrated.

Finally the Doctor let her go and they just grinned at each other for a moment, then they both began speaking at once, stopped, started again at exactly the same moment and then stopped again, laughing.

'You first, then,' Rose said finally.

'No, no…' insisted the Doctor, 'you carry on.'

'Actually I don't know quite where to begin,' Rose confessed.

The Doctor threw a look in the direction of Rez, who was standing around looking a little embarrassed at the overt display of affection.

'How about starting with introducing the new boyfriend?' suggested the Doctor with a grin.

'This is Rez,' Rose said, ignoring the Doctor's teasing. 'He's a human living with the locals,' she added.

'Pleased to meet you,' said the Doctor, extending a hand for the lad to shake.

Rez looked a little hesitant.

'Does he shake?' he asked, raising an eyebrow at Rose.

She and Rez exchanged a knowing look and then both of them burst into hysterics.

'I'll take that as a no, shall I?' The Doctor sounded a little hurt.

Rose managed to stop herself laughing and apologised. 'Private joke,' she explained.

If anything this only made him look more upset.

'So, are you going to introduce us to *your* new friend?' she asked, grinning, and nodded over the Doctor's shoulder in the direction of a severe-looking woman in her fifties who was walking purposefully towards them.

'Let me introduce the commander of this fine ship, Professor Petra Shulough,' said the Doctor. 'Professor, this is my travelling companion, Rose Tyler, and this is, er, her new friend, Rez.'

The professor nodded at the newcomers but her expression remained serious. 'You live with the natives?' she asked Rez.

He nodded. 'I was found here as a baby in an escape pod fifteen years ago.'

'An orphan!' exclaimed the professor, and Rose thought she could detect an unexpected emotion in the woman's voice. Was it empathy?

'And you've been brought up as a native since then?'

Again he nodded.

The professor seemed to be making an effort to stifle whatever emotional reaction she was having and her voice hardened. 'So what can you tell us about the creatures that attacked us last night?'

'Creatures?'

'Big hairy chaps with four arms and serious talons,' the Doctor said, giving Rez some more details.

'Snap!' said Rose.

'You've seen them too?' The Doctor sounded excited.

Rose affected an air of nonchalance. 'Been there, seen that, bought the T-shirt.' She grinned again.

'You were attacked too?' asked the professor, surprised at this development.

'Our village was raided last night,' explained Rez.

'But it was OK,' Rose hurried to tell the Doctor. 'I saw them off with a hot drink!'

'I'm sorry?'

Rose was pleased to hear the surprise in the Doctor's voice.

'I threw my drink at them and it seemed to stop them. Like Superman and kryptonite.'

'You found a weakness!' The Doctor was impressed.

Rose was chuffed. The score was now two-nil, Rose told herself.

'I think we need to compare notes,' the Doctor decided, and started to lead them back towards the spaceship. 'And talking of hot drinks, any chance of a cup of tea, Professor?'

* * *

Hespell was on guard duty. Not that there was much to guard – the creature still seemed unconscious. Most humans would recover from a stun charge like that in a matter of hours, but you never could tell with aliens. Or so he'd heard. Hespell hadn't actually met many aliens. Humans from distant colonies, yes, but not many real count-the-eyes, freaky aliens.

He pulled out his EntPad and started playing one of his favourite games. It was a classic shoot-'em-up adventure, a real retro gaming experience without even the most primitive kind of virtual neural feedback, but it was still pretty exciting. Well, more exciting than doing nothing anyway. Within minutes he was totally absorbed in the game's fictional scenario, sending his team of avatars out on the first stage of their quest.

Behind him, unnoticed, the hairy beast's eyelids began to twitch. It was beginning to awaken at last.

Rez was finding it difficult to keep up. Both the Doctor and Rose had been speaking nineteen to the dozen since they'd met up and it was giving him a headache. So, ignoring them, he turned his attention to his surroundings. The sky boat was everything he had imagined it would be: full of strange electrical sounds and magical machines. It was the most advanced technological thing he had ever seen and yet, despite the very alien nature of everything around him, he found it strangely comforting. It was almost as if he was meant to be part of this world. Perhaps the ship he'd been born on had been something like this.

Rez didn't often spend much time thinking about his origins. He still had the remains of his escape pod, the keepsakes and the mysterious cube that had been placed in it with him, but that was all he had of his life before Laylora and that was all he wanted. If he stopped and thought about the mother and father who had put him into that pod he got upset, even though he had no idea about who those people might have been. He had concluded long ago that speculation was pointless and, anyway, the only person who deserved the title 'mother' was Jaelette, who had taken him in. The Tribe of the Three Valleys were the only family he had ever known.

Leaving the Doctor and Rose to catch up, Professor Shulough had joined Rez, who was staring into space.

'How did a human teenager come to be on this planet, then?' she asked.

He told her his story, but she seemed more interested in the tribe and the planet than in what had happened to him. She asked him lots of questions about the way they lived and how the planet provided for them, and seemed fascinated by the answers he gave. The professor must be a few years older than Mother Jaelette, thought Rez, but she was nothing like her. He couldn't imagine anyone being comforted by a cuddle with this woman. She seemed so cold and distant.

Underneath her severe exterior, however, Petra Shulough found herself strangely intrigued by the young man. Something in his story resonated deep inside the most private part of her being. Was it some long-buried maternal instinct? She doubted it; she'd never been conscious of a desire to parent before.

So what was it? She had never been very good at expressing herself emotionally – she preferred to keep people at a safe distance – but as she listened to the young man speaking about his life, she felt an urge to reach out and hold him tight. She found herself wondering what it had been like for him to grow up among aliens, cut off from his own people. It must have been so hard. She knew there was no loneliness quite like that of an orphan.

Cross with herself for thinking like this, she took a deep breath and tried to concentrate on the facts. This boy represented an opportunity; a unique resource. His knowledge and his experiences could be the key to confirming that this was Guillan's paradise.

'So what's the story with these monsters, then?' Rose was asking the Doctor.

'I don't know,' he confessed. 'At least not yet.'

'Not run into them before?'

'I don't think they're the travelling kind,' he murmured, deep in thought. Suddenly he snapped out of it. 'What was this drink, then?'

The sudden gear change threw Rose. Annoyed with

herself, she asked, 'What drink?' like a total amateur.

'This jinnera stuff. You said it stopped the creature.'

'Yeah, it certainly seemed to… like they were allergic or something.'

The Doctor leapt up from his seat and dashed across the room to where the professor was interrogating Rez. 'The jinnen plant – can you show me?'

'Of course,' replied Rez.

Luckily it didn't take Rez long to find a jinnen bush, heavy with fruit, not too far from the spaceship. He showed the Doctor the leaves they used to brew their hot drink, the peach-like fruit, which they ate, and the seeds of the fruit, which, when dried, were used to make a sleeping potion.

'What an incredibly useful plant,' commented the Doctor, impressed.

'Laylora provides,' replied Rez automatically.

'Does she really? That's very convenient…'

The Doctor turned to Kendle, who had insisted on accompanying them into the forest. 'I take it you have lab facilities on board?'

Kendle nodded.

The Doctor gathered a handful of the leaves and the fruit, then stood up. 'Let's find out what makes this stuff tick, shall we?'

A short time later work was under way in the spaceship's laboratory. At least it was for the Doctor.

Rose had been relegated to the position of observer. The Doctor was slicing up bits of the jinnen plant and its fruit, subjecting them to various pieces of testing equipment. It was all a long way from any science Rose had done at school, and she felt a bit annoyed at the lack of explanation that the Doctor was giving her.

'Anything I can do?' she asked for the umpteenth time, hoping that she could at least pass him things, like a good assistant, but apparently even that was asking too much.

'Not really,' the Doctor said, carefully adding a lumpy mass of pulverised jinnen seed to a beaker of hot water. 'Why don't you take a wander around the ship? I think the professor was going to show your friend around…'

Rose could see that there was little advantage in hanging around here, counting test tubes. The Doctor was in his element, playing the mad scientist, but that really wasn't Rose's thing. She was more of a people person. She decided to take his advice and have a look around.

The *Humphrey Bogart* wasn't that large a ship (at least not compared to the TARDIS) and Rose managed to find her way to the bridge without too much trouble. When she got there she could see the professor and Kendle but there was no sign of Rez. The two of them were deep in discussion, so she waited at the open door, not wanting to interrupt. Neither of them could see her and, although Rose didn't like to eavesdrop, she couldn't help hearing what they were saying.

'There's nothing in the book about creatures like those things,' Kendle was insisting.

'But that doesn't mean this isn't the planet,' replied the professor, with equal certainty. 'Look at the evidence. The size matches, the atmosphere's right, the gravity. The name. It all adds up.'

Kendle shrugged. 'There are lots of Earth-like planets out there. You know the statistics. Planets with essentially the same properties as Earth are common throughout known space. And more than one planet can share a name.'

'OK, I agree it's possible that another planet in the same area could have been given the same name, but I still think that this is the one the *Armstrong* found. This has to be the Paradise Planet that Guillan discovered.'

Kendle shook his head. 'It's no paradise. Guillan said the planet he found was totally in balance. Its ecosystem was perfect. Right?'

Shulough nodded. 'You don't need to tell me what's in that journal. I know it by heart.'

'The Doctor was talking to the boy when we were outside looking for the plant. He said that things have been bad on this planet recently, earthquakes and floods, wild weather... Doesn't sound very benevolent to me.'

The professor was unimpressed. 'Oh yes, Rez said something about that to me too, but that's just native superstition surely. It doesn't mean anything.'

Rose could see that the argument was going to run and run, so she decided not to interrupt. Instead she backtracked down the corridor and set about exploring for herself. Rez must be around here somewhere.

Rez was already on level nine of the game, much to Hespell's chagrin. The boy had found him playing on his EntPad and had instantly wanted to have a go himself. Hespell had shown him the basic controls, not expecting him to have much success, but Rez had taken to it like a duck to water.

As Hespell looked on, with increasing disbelief, Rez had raced through the basic levels of the game and was now close to matching, if not overtaking, Hespell's own best performance.

Hespell sighed, wondering if he'd ever get a chance to have another go himself.

Ania Baker, the young crew member who had been injured in the second Witiku attack, had joined the Doctor in the laboratory. Ania explained to him that she was getting bored lying on her own in the MedLab and wanted to help, but the Doctor suspected that it was other company she was really after, not his.

'Isn't Jonn here?' she'd asked when she came into the room, adding, 'I mean Hespell,' by way of further clarification.

The Doctor told her that her friend was guarding the captured creature and noted with some amusement the slight blush on the young woman's face at his use of the word 'friend'. He then asked her to help him transfer the finished jinnen solution into the various containers they had managed to assemble.

'How does this work?' she said, watching the brown liquid fill a plastic container.

'Are you a scientist?'

The young woman shook her head. 'Not really. Navigation is my field. But I'm curious.'

The Doctor smiled. 'Nothing wrong with curiosity.'

'So what does this stuff do?'

'If it works, it should stop the creatures in their tracks.'

'But will it kill them?'

The Doctor looked away.

'You don't know the answer, do you?'

He turned back to her and met her gaze. 'Not entirely, no. But I'm hoping it won't be fatal. I want something to use defensively. I don't want to kill unless I have to. We know it had a noticeable effect on the Witiku in a small dose, so I'm hoping a much larger amount will have an even greater effect. There's only one way to find out, though. We need to test it.'

Baker realised what the Doctor was suggesting. 'You want to try it on the creature we caught?'

'Of course not. That would be cruel and dangerous. No, we need to take a cell sample from the creature and use the liquid on that.'

The Doctor looked around and started picking up bits of equipment.

'What are you doing?'

'Well, I don't think we're going to get the patient in here, do you? So we'd better take what we need to the cargo bay and do our little experiment there.'

'Boys!' sighed Rose as she walked through the cargo-bay doors and found the pair of them absorbed in their game. Neither the crewman nor Rez acknowledged her presence. She walked up behind them and tried to get a look at the playing field, which was a football-sized hologram projected from the device. Inside the hologram she could see a number of zombie creatures, which Rez appeared to be shooting at. Rose shook her head. The more things change, the more they stay the same, she thought. It was obvious that she wouldn't get any sense out of them until the game was over, so she wandered across to take a closer look at their prisoner.

Lying on its back, chained to the floor, the thing which Rez had called a Witiku didn't look quite as frightening as it had last night, but Rose was still nervous to be this close. The chains holding it in place were heavy and it didn't look very comfortable. She found herself feeling sorry for the poor creature. In the cold light of day it seemed more of an animal and less of a monster. Something sparkling on its chest caught her eye – could it be some of the jewels that the villagers wore? Leaning over, Rose gave it a closer examination. It *was* one of the necklaces that the Laylorans all wore and, furthermore, Rose was fairly sure that she had seen one just like this before, although she couldn't pinpoint exactly where.

While she was trying to remember, she noticed that the creature's chest was rising and falling in a new rhythm. But before she could react, its whole body suddenly buckled, knocking her off balance and causing her to fall face first into its hairy chest. With a roar of fury, the creature stopped pretending to be asleep and pulled at the chains with each of its four arms. For Rose it was like being on a bucking bronco, as the creature used all its strength to yank at the bonds. To her horror, the chains were not up to the strain. They twisted and then snapped simultaneously. The creature sent her flying as it stumbled to its feet.

Rose found herself colliding with Hespell, who was reaching for his weapon. The two of them fell in a heap on the floor. Rez dropped the EntPad and backed against the nearest wall as the creature moved towards him.

Rose looked around to see where Hespell's weapon had fallen. Her heart sank as she saw that it had skidded right across the room. The Witiku was moving towards Rez, who looked petrified. Its talons sprang out from the back of each paw and it raised its highest arms, ready to strike.

Rose rolled to her feet. 'Oi, what about me, then?' she called, and managed to distract it momentarily before it changed course and headed towards her. So much for that plan.

Rose backed away in the direction of the weapon that Hespell had dropped. Her foot hit something hard and, without taking her eyes off the creature lurching towards her, she squatted and reached down. Unfortunately for her, it wasn't the weapon – it was the end of one of the broken chains and was no use at all. The Witiku swiped one of its arms at her and Rose jerked back just in time to feel the edge of the talon brush through the ends of her hair.

Suddenly the doors opened and the Doctor was there. Even in her vulnerable state, Rose felt a sudden burst of hope. The Doctor was guaranteed to sort it out. Scrambling backwards, like some kind of human crab, she realised that the Doctor didn't seem to have a weapon. Instead he had his arms full of what looked like laboratory equipment. Behind him the female crew member, Baker, was carrying a large plastic container full of some brown liquid.

'Change of plan,' announced the Doctor, and threw the armful of equipment in the path of the Witiku. But the creature just batted it away with its four arms and kept coming.

Baker tossed the container of liquid to the Doctor. 'Try this,' she suggested.

The Doctor looked torn, not wanting to harm the

Witiku if he could avoid it.

'Doctor!' Rose urged him, ducking out of the way of another swipe of claws.

She was backed into a corner now, with no way to escape. The Doctor had no choice but to act.

'Sorry, fella,' he muttered as he tore the cap off the container and threw the contents at it.

The creature screamed as the liquid hit him, then fell to the floor. Rose was also splashed with the liquid, which is when she realised that she wasn't being soaked by water.

'It's jinnera!' she gasped.

The creature was still on the floor, screaming.

The Doctor looked pained. 'I wanted to test it on a cell sample first,' he explained.

Rose understood. 'You didn't have a choice,' she told him.

Baker helped Hespell get to his feet. Across the room Rez groaned and clutched at his head.

'Look!' cried Baker, pointing at the creature, which was still lying on the floor but was now shaking like a leaf and its hair seemed to be shrinking.

The Witiku continued to react to the soaking it had received. As they watched, amazed, the creature began to change right in front of them. Its hair retracted and its whole body shrank. It became man-sized.

With a sudden burst of inspiration, Rose realised what was happening.

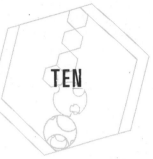

TEN

'The Witiku – they're the missing people!' Rose announced.

Even as she said it the transformation of the Witiku that had been captured was complete. A confused, dazed and naked Brother Hugan was lying on the floor. The Doctor hurried forward and gave the poor man his coat to preserve what little dignity he had.

Ania Baker was open-mouthed at what she had seen.

'How is that possible?' she asked. 'How can something change its form like that?'

Rose glanced at the Doctor and smiled to herself. 'Oh, you'd be surprised,' she muttered.

'There are more things in heaven and earth,' started the Doctor, before stopping himself mid-quotation. 'Sorry, channelling old Will again. Bad habit.'

The Layloran shaman was still looking pale and shaky. He didn't seem to know where he was.

'Brother Hugan! Are you all right?' Rez asked him

urgently, his concern overcoming the shock and fear of the last few minutes.

Brother Hugan did not answer, but just stared into space, shivering uncontrollably.

The Doctor looked at Rez with a serious expression. 'I'm sorry. I don't think he's very well at all… Let's get him to the MedLab.'

The medical computers hummed happily and the read-out screens showed that the vital signs were normal, in so far as Professor Shulough could tell what normal was for the natives of this planet.

'How is he?' asked the Doctor, who was looking on with interest.

Ten minutes had passed since they'd brought the shaman into the MedLab and so far there was no sign that the attention he was receiving was having any effect.

'He'll live,' she told him coolly, before turning away to deal with what she considered more interesting matters.

Rose saw the Doctor bristle and knew that he was biting his tongue. This Professor Shulough was a cold fish all right and Rose had taken an instant dislike to her.

'How did you know the jinnera would have that effect?' the professor demanded.

'I didn't, it was just a theory based on Rose's observation.' The Doctor winked at Rose.

'When the Witiku attacked the village I threw my

drink at one of them and it reacted badly,' she explained.

'Do you make a habit of throwing drinks at people?' asked the professor sarcastically.

Rose shot her a dark look.

'So I brewed up a little solution and, when the creature threatened to escape, we used it,' continued the Doctor, ignoring the interruption, 'and now we know where all these monsters are coming from.' He smiled, pleased with their progress.

The professor still wanted more answers. 'But why is it happening?'

The Doctor thrust his hands into his pockets. 'Why? Oh, why can come later. Right now the important thing is that we've got a way to deal with the creatures. And not just a weapon, a cure.'

'You think it's some kind of illness?' asked Rose.

'Not as such, no. I was talking metaphorically,' he told her, 'although now you come to mention it, maybe it is some kind of disease.'

He stopped and frowned, running through the possibilities. There was something else, something he wasn't getting. Then, with a quick shake of his head, he left the problem to tick over at the back of his mind and returned to the present.

'First things first,' he announced. 'We need to get a whole lot of this jinnera stuff made up. Trouble is, there don't seem to be that many bushes in this area of the forest,' he added.

Rez, who had been standing over at Brother Hugan's bedside, watching the old man sleep, cleared his throat. 'I might be able to help you there,' he told them. 'We use jinnen for so many things, we've huge stockpiles of it in the village.'

On the bridge of the *Humphrey Bogart*, Kendle was checking the progress of the ship's auto-repair systems. Everything seemed to be coming along nicely. The doors at the rear of the bridge opened and Professor Shulough appeared.

'Another twelve hours and we should be able to take off. But without some trisilicate we won't get very far,' he told her.

This didn't seem to be what the professor wanted to hear. 'Then we'd better confirm now one way or another whether this is Guillan's paradise. If it is Laylora, trisilicate shouldn't be a problem,' she reminded him. She then said that she was intending to visit the village with the Doctor, Rose and the human boy, Rez.

Kendle, as conscious of security as ever, didn't think this was a good idea. 'It might be dangerous. I think I should come with you.'

The professor shook her head. 'There's no need. The Doctor's made up some more jinnen solution – enough to deal with those creatures if we should run into any.'

'OK, but be careful,' he insisted.

Sadly, he watched her leave the bridge. What had happened to the bright-eyed young woman he remembered so vividly on her graduation day? He shook his head slowly. It was no good thinking about the past; that Petra Shulough was long gone. And in his heart he knew why.

Trying to put his concerns about the professor out of his mind, he turned back to the job in hand. He just hoped she would find what she was really looking for. Whatever that was.

Rez had been left alone in the MedLab, to keep an eye on the recovering shaman. The old Layloran was sleeping more peacefully now and some colour had returned to his cheeks. Rez hoped he was going to be all right. The tribe needed him more than ever in the present crisis, even if his ideas were a little old-fashioned.

Across the room was the bed that had, until recently, been occupied by the other patient, the female crew member called Baker. Thinking about what had happened to her, he now felt a terrible guilt. It had been one of the Witiku that had nearly killed her and that meant one of his tribe. How could a Layloran be turned into a creature like that? It seemed like magic, the sort of mystical event that Brother Hugan was always talking about, but Rez couldn't believe in stuff like that. Especially here in this spaceship, surrounded by high technology. And yet... he had witnessed it with his own eyes: one moment it had been a Witiku, one of Laylora's legendary guardians, the next it had been Brother Hugan. Had this kind of transformation happened before in the distant past? Was that the source of the legends?

Brother Hugan coughed and opened his eyes.

Rez turned to give him his full attention. 'How are you?' he asked anxiously.

The old man's eyes flickered around the room, panicky.

'It's all right,' Rez assured him. 'You're safe now.' He gripped the old man's hand and was shocked at how frail it felt. How could it have been a massive taloned paw before?

The old man's lips were moving but no sound was coming out. Rez leaned closer to the old man's mouth. 'Water,' he croaked in a parched whisper.

Rez looked around the room – there was no sign of a jug of any kind. But he remembered seeing Rose get water from somewhere – one of the machines, but which one? He crossed the room to where Rose had been standing. It must have been on this side of the room, he thought. And then, without warning, something exploded on the back of his head and he fell to the ground.

Professor Shulough found the door to her quarters open and frowned. She was sure she'd left it locked, as she alway did. Moving cautiously into the room, she discovered the reason for her confusion. It was the Doctor. He and the girl Rose were looking through her paradise collection – all the artefacts and bits of evidence that she had accumulated during her search.

'Don't you understand the concept of privacy?' she asked, but if she was hoping to surprise the stranger she was sorely disappointed.

He glanced up, as if he'd been waiting for her, and then looked back at the flight report he'd found. 'Ah, there you are. Ready to go, are we?'

The professor grabbed the sketchbook that Rose was looking at and dropped it back into its folder. 'Do you mind? This is private,' she insisted.

'Sorry,' said Rose. 'We were only looking.'

'Clues,' explained the Doctor, rather obliquely. 'Is this all the stuff you have on the so-called Paradise Planet?'

'Yes, and it's taken me years and a small fortune to bring it all together. I'm not about to start sharing it now.' Angrily, she snatched the flight records from the Doctor's grasp.

He looked up and smiled innocently. 'But you think you've solved the mystery, don't you? You think this is the Paradise Planet that Guillan found?'

The professor swallowed hard as the Doctor's intense brown eyes seemed to bore deep inside her. He was a hard man to argue with.

'I think so, yes.'

'So what does all this matter now? It's academic if this is the place you have been looking for.'

She couldn't fault the logic of that.

'But if this stuff does relate to this planet,' continued the Doctor, pausing to flash a grin at her, 'then it might just tell us something about what's going on with the shape-shifting locals and all that.'

Rose frowned. 'They're shape-shifters?'

'Well, no, not as such. Not in the classic sense,' admitted the Doctor. 'Not like your Axon or your Zygon, or any other gon come to that...'

Rose gave the professor a sympathetic look – he was off again, blithering.

'But they did change shape, or transform,' continued the Doctor, getting back to the point, 'and I for one would like to know why.'

'And have you found anything?' asked the professor levelly.

The Doctor's face fell. 'No,' he admitted. 'So let's try plan B.'

Rose smiled. 'There's a plan B?' she teased him, sounding surprised. 'That makes a change.'

'There's a plan C too,' he murmured in a slightly menacing way, 'which involves taking you home and leaving you with your mother for a couple of weeks, so don't push it!' And then he was off, his long legs propelling him to the door at most people's jogging speed. 'Come on, then. Let's go and see the natives. I hear they're friendly.'

And at that point, as if to throw doubt on his assertion, Rez appeared staggering down the corridor, clutching the back of his head.

'What happened to you?' asked Rose, worried.

'Brother Hugan,' he replied simply.

The Doctor was concerned. 'He hit you?'

Rez nodded and then instantly winced, the sudden movement doing nothing for the state of his head, which was throbbing with pain. 'Hit me and then ran off.'

'Right,' said the Doctor commandingly. 'Let's get you something for that headache and then we'd better go after him, before he does anything stupid.'

'This might sting a bit,' warned the professor as she dabbed at the back of his head with a medicated cleansing wipe.

Rez winced. She wasn't wrong.

'I'll put a dressing on it,' she told him. 'It'll speed up the healing.'

Rez looked at the professor as she searched through the cabinet for a bandage. For the first time since he had met her he was seeing something akin to a caring side. Perhaps his initial evaluation had been too harsh.

'Thank you,' he said with genuine gratitude as she gently fixed the dressing in place with a spray of instant plaster.

'You're young, fit. You'll recover from this in no time.' She smiled and looked suddenly much younger. 'You must have been through much worse, living alone among aliens.'

Rez shrugged. 'I never really thought about it,' he said.

The professor raised a quizzical eyebrow. 'Never?' she asked, not really believing him. 'Are you telling me you never stop and think about where you came from? You realise you must have family somewhere...'

'Maybe not never,' he confessed. 'But what's the point? My life is here. Whatever world I came from before I was sent here... it's lost to me for ever.'

Not now, thought the professor, but she kept the thought to herself as Rez jumped down from the examination table he had been perched on.

'Am I OK to go?' he asked.

The professor nodded. 'Sure. Let's get on the trail of your shaman.'

In the forest Brother Hugan was running like the wind, driven by the voice in his head. Laylora was calling to him. She needed him to act. The humans were killing her with their very presence, only Brother Hugan could help her. That's why she had chosen him to take the form of the Witiku. And why he had been chosen again to do her bidding.

Ignoring the branches and ferns that whipped his body as he ran recklessly through the trees, Brother Hugan felt an enormous joy. At last his studies had been justified. The ancient Laylorans had known their own world well and that wisdom had been all but lost. Brother Hugan alone had kept the sacred flame of that knowledge alight and now, at last, he had been rewarded for this loyalty. He knew what he had to do. He had to rouse his people and lead them in battle against the enemy. The aliens and their stinking, dirty technology must be removed from the planet by force. Laylora must be cleansed.

Oblivious to anything else, Brother Hugan ran on, a man possessed.

The Doctor was following the trail of the escaping shaman.

'It looks like he's heading in the same direction we are,' he observed.

'But aren't the tribe at the temple?' asked Rose. 'We took shelter there from the Witiku attack.'

'They will have returned to the village by now,' Rez told her. 'Life must go on.'

'But surely the creatures could attack again? They could take more of you off and create more Witiku. Another couple of nights like last night and there will be more of the creatures than there are villagers.'

The Doctor shook his head, dismissing Rose's analysis. 'No, that won't happen. I won't let it.'

Rose knew that tone in his voice. It was calm and cool but hard as iron. No second chances.

The four of them hurried on through the forest, Rez leading the way, followed by Rose and then the Doctor and Professor Shulough bringing up the rear. The Doctor dropped back to fall into step alongside the professor.

'What's it all about, then, this quest of yours?' he asked, without preamble.

She looked at him sideways with a degree of suspicion.

'You know what it's about. I've been searching for the Paradise Planet,' she replied.

'Oh, I know what you've been doing,' he went on cheerfully, 'but I want to know *why*.'

'Why does anyone do anything?'

'The usual reasons: fame, money, love… But you've spent years on this quest, and a fair bit of cash too, I'd say, although I'd steer clear of whoever sold you that ship in the future – I reckon the mileage clock's been reset on that one, if you know what I mean… But my point is…' He trailed off, having taken himself down a cul-de-sac for once. 'What is my point?' He pondered for a moment and then continued with renewed vigour: 'Oh yes, you. And your quest. Because that's what it is, isn't it? A good old-fashioned quest.'

The professor shrugged. 'I suppose so.'

The Doctor shook his head. 'Nah, come off it. You can't fool me. This is something big, isn't it? Like a grail quest… Hold on, that's it, isn't it? It's not the object of the classic quest that matters, it's the journey itself that's important.'

Pleased with himself, the Doctor was almost bouncing along the path. The professor, meanwhile, just regarded him with cold eyes.

'What kind of doctor are you? Some kind of shrink?

I don't need a psychiatrist,' she told him firmly.

'I'm just interested, that's all.'

'Well, find a new hobby to take up!' she spat back at him, and with that she extended her stride and moved ahead of the Doctor, curtailing any further conversation.

The Doctor watched as she strode ahead purposefully, trying to figure her out. There was something there. Underneath all the bluster and hardness there was a human heart beating inside that woman, he was sure of it. He'd seen the way she had reacted to Rez. Something about the orphan's story had touched her, he was sure of it.

At first glance when they reached the village everything looked normal, but then Rosc realised that everyone was busy repairing torn tents or cleaning up debris. The Witiku attack had come before they'd had a chance to fully recover from the earth tremor, so there was plenty to be done. All the villagers who had escaped to the temple ruins last night seemed to have returned and they appeared determined to get back to normality as quickly as possible.

Mother Jaelette and Kaylen were the first to greet them, welcoming Rez home with big hugs. They were polite but less enthusiastic in their greetings to Rose and her companions. Rose introduced the Doctor and the professor and told the Laylorans that they had both come to help. Rose was giving the professor the benefit of the doubt here, but hoped she wouldn't be proved wrong. Rez began to tell them about Brother Hugan but they stopped him.

'We already know,' Kaylen told him. 'He's in his tent. He came back a little while ago.'

'How is he?' demanded the Doctor.

Mother Jaelette looked worried. 'He was babbling incoherently, making no sense at all. We tried to calm him down and get him to talk to us, but he just collapsed. We've put him in his tent and given him water, but he's no better.'

The Doctor asked to be taken to see him, explaining that he needed urgent medical attention. Kaylen and Rez accompanied him immediately, leaving Rose and the professor with Mother Jaelette.

The two older women regarded each other with suspicion. Rose felt that Friday night feeling, the one you get when somebody knocks over a drink or calls the wrong girl something unpleasant and you just know there'll be a nasty silence that can only end in a fight.

'Well, this is nice,' she said brightly, hoping to defuse the moment without the need for violence.

'Your sky boat landed in our forest,' said Mother Jaelette eventually.

'A forced landing,' replied the professor. 'The damage was limited.'

'Not to the forest!'

'I meant to the ship,' stated the professor, cool as ever.

'The forest is more important than your sky boat,' Mother Jaelette threw back at her.

Rose knew she had to break this apart. She was sure this wasn't the way first contact was meant to go.

'Look, we can see you've got a lot on right now,' she started, addressing the tribeswoman. 'Why don't we –' she gestured at the professor inclusively – 'have a wander round, get out of your hair, eh?'

It seemed for a moment as if Mother Jaelette wanted to do something a little more permanent than removing the human from her hair, but she took the opportunity Rose was offering her and withdrew.

'I do have things to do,' she conceded. 'Try not to get in anyone's way.' And then she was gone.

Rose let out a sigh of relief. 'That wasn't a barrel of laughs, was it?' she said, but the professor just shrugged and moved off. Rose hurried after her. Somebody had to try and keep the moody cow out of trouble and it looked as if Rose had been volunteered for the task.

'Fascinating jewellery,' observed the professor after they had been walking around the village for a short while.

'Yeah, amazing, isn't it?' said Rose, glad to hear something approaching enthusiasm in the woman's voice for once.

'Can those really be trisilicate crystals?'

'I dunno. Here, have a look at one.'

Rose fished the crystal she'd picked up at the temple

out of her jeans pocket and tossed it at the professor, who weighed it in her hands, then produced a pocket magnifying glass and started to examine it in more detail.

'This is incredible. It's perfect.'

'Yeah,' said Rose, affecting a casual attitude. 'Apparently they're a real problem for the natives, mucking up their fields and all that.'

'They're abundant?' asked the professor, matching Rose for casualness now.

'You can say that again!' Rose grinned. 'They've got a pile in one room under that ruined temple place. I couldn't believe what I was seeing.'

Alarmingly, the professor took her arm, like they were old friends or something. 'Can you show me?' she asked, moving her mouth into an unfamiliar shape.

Rose realised with a start that the woman was trying to smile! She looked over in the direction of the shaman's tent but there was no sign of the Doctor.

'Don't worry about them. We won't be long,' the professor urged her.

'I should just tell him where we're going,' Rose insisted.

The professor sighed and nodded. 'OK, then, if you have to.'

Inside the shaman's brightly decorated tent the Doctor and Rez were with Brother Hugan. That is, they were inside the tent with the old man, but to what extent he was actually there was open to debate. He was rolling back and forth on his sleeping blankets, sweating and shivering in equal measure. And all the time he was muttering about Laylora.

'Laylora demands… Laylora needs cleansing…' The words kept tumbling out, hardly audible.

Rez looked to the Doctor, willing him to do something, but the stranger in the brown coat just stuffed his hands into his pockets and shuffled around, looking concerned.

'I think the poor bloke's lost his mind,' he speculated. 'A side effect of becoming a Witiku.'

'So will this happen to the rest of the missing, when we find them and give them the cure?' Rez asked, alarmed.

The Doctor didn't meet his eyes when he replied. 'I really don't know. Not necessarily. I hope.' And behind his back he crossed his fingers.

The tent flap was pushed open and Kaylen appeared with a steaming cup of jinnera.

'Are you sure this is a good idea?' she asked as she handed the cup to the Doctor.

The Doctor shrugged. 'You said you used this stuff to help you relax, didn't you? I think that's just what this poor bloke needs to do right now.'

Rez still looked doubtful. 'But the last time he went near the stuff he didn't exactly relax, did he?' he said, remembering what he had seen earlier that day.

'But he was a Witiku then. Now he's back in his own natural form. And to you Laylorans, this is the original Horlicks, right?'

He winked at Kaylen, who had no idea what he was talking about. She took a hasty step back, as if worried that the twitch in his eye might be catching.

The Doctor bent down by the side of the shaman. 'Here, help me get him into a sitting position,' he said.

Rez hurried across and a moment later the Doctor was able to raise the cup of jinnera to the old man's lips. He drank and almost choked in his enthusiasm.

'Steady on, old fella. There's no rush,' muttered the Doctor, but a moment later the man lurched violently backwards and then forward again, spitting out all of the liquid he'd swallowed.

The Doctor and Rez both jumped backwards instinctively, giving the shaman the opportunity to leap up and push them both back on their heels. Brother Hugan then rushed towards the tent flap. Kaylen made a half-hearted attempt to stop him, but he just tossed her to one side, back into the path of the Doctor and Rez. In a moment he was out of the tent and away.

By the time the Doctor, Rez and Kaylen had disentangled themselves from the pile of arms and legs they had collapsed into, the shaman was long gone. They rushed out of the tent and tried to see which way he had gone, but there was no sign of him. He had disappeared completely.

They were still frantically looking a moment or two later when Rose and the professor joined them. Rose began to tell the Doctor about wanting to take the professor to the temple.

The Doctor suddenly clicked his fingers. 'The temple! Of course, that's where he'll be heading.'

'Rose and I can go and look for him,' the professor said quickly, to everyone's surprise. 'You need to get the jinnen back to the ship to make up a batch of Witiku cure, don't you? While you do that, we can find the shaman.'

'I'll go with them,' volunteered Rez.

The professor shook her head. 'You should be careful with that head wound of yours,' she said. 'You need rest.'

Rez insisted that he was fine now, but the Doctor, who had been considering the situation for a moment, decided he wanted Rez to help him.

'Rose can look after the professor, can't you, Rose?' he said, looking Rose in the eye. She was about to argue, but the Doctor gave her a sly wink – he needed her to do this for him. 'But take care,' he added, 'Brother Hugan's not himself and the rest of the Witiku must be round here somewhere.'

Rose nodded, accepting her mission, and set off with the professor.

The Doctor looked at Rez and Kaylen. 'Come on, then. Where's all this jinnen you promised me?'

ELEVEN

It struck Rose that the days couldn't be very long on Laylora because it was already getting dark as she and the professor set off from the village. Rez had given her instructions on how to find the temple and the ruins, but she was beginning to be able to recognise the path through the trees now. The professor had set off at a brisk walking pace but had soon slowed down in the heat of the late afternoon sun.

The forest was alive with life. Not just the plants, which were vibrant and sweet-smelling, but insects and animals too. There were little midges, but they were less irritating than any Rose had ever encountered before and didn't seem interested in biting her. There were also some beautiful butterfly-like creatures that flitted about between the bushes and flowers. And above them was a canopy of leafy branches, through which the sun burst in mottled patterns. The air was filled with the songs of numerous birds. Rose couldn't help but smile as they walked though this sensual delight.

The professor, striding alongside her, didn't seem to be interested in her surroundings; she just wanted to get to the ruins of the ancient temple as quickly as possible. Couldn't she appreciate the beauty of this place? In the end Rose asked the woman straight out.

'Beauty fades,' was the professor's only reply.

This made Rose study the woman's lined face again. Had she once been beautiful herself? She had good cheekbones and perfectly balanced features – it was certainly possible that she'd been a looker when she was younger. Still could be, if she'd just chill a little and smile occasionally.

The professor looked up at the darkening sky. 'Sun's going down. We should get a move on.'

Rose stepped forward to lead the way. 'We'd better take care, though,' she warned. 'We don't want to frighten him.'

'Who?' asked the professor, confused.

'Brother Hugan, of course.' Rose was surprised. Had she forgotten the reason for their journey?

They moved on into the gathering shadows.

Petra Shulough glanced at the young woman beside her. She envied Rose her confidence – she seemed utterly devoid of doubt and fear. One of the great freedoms of being young, she supposed. Just like the boy Rez.

As she followed Rose through the trees, the professor was aware of a strange feeling of emptiness coming over her. The trisilicate had been the final piece of the jigsaw; now there was no doubt that this was indeed the planet that Guillan had found... Guillan and her parents. But somehow the knowledge that she had succeeded in her quest was not giving her the satisfaction that she had expected. Instead of joy she just felt numb.

Her mind kept going back to the teenage orphan. Like Petra, Rez had lost his parents at an early age, but he had never really known them. What must it have been like for him, abandoned as a baby and brought up by aliens? Had this been a paradise for him?

Elsewhere in the forest the Doctor, Rez and Kaylen were arriving back at the spaceship, each of them carrying bags of the heavy jinnen seed.

'Shame you lot haven't invented the wheelbarrow,' muttered the Doctor as they came in sight of the crashed ship.

To his delight, as they got closer Hespell came out of the airlock to give them a hand. With him was Ania Baker, who was now looking in much better health than when he had last seen her. She seemed to be over the shock of witnessing the Witiku's transformation and back to her normal bubbly self.

'Feeling better?' asked the Doctor, pleased to see that his patient was out and about.

'Much better,' she said, returning his smile. 'Thanks to you.'

The Doctor noted the way she was standing very close to the red-haired lad. He thought it was sweet; the long-limbed and slightly awkward Hespell and the tiny, precise Baker would make a nice couple. He hoped they'd have the chance to become one.

While Hespell and Baker started taking the jinnen to the lab, the Doctor sought out Kendle. As expected, the ex-marine was on the bridge, alone.

'Did you get what you went for?' he asked, as the Doctor joined him.

'I think so. But have you managed to rig some suitable delivery systems? The solution will be no good as a cure if we can't control the dosage.'

Kendle shrugged. 'There were some bits and pieces of cleaning equipment that I've managed to make something out of,' he told the Doctor. 'Do you really think spraying the creatures with this stuff will turn them back to their native form?'

The Doctor pulled a face. 'That's the theory.'

He leaned over Kendle's console and scanned the information on the screen. 'Talking of theories – oh, systems at 95 per cent, that's good… Where was I? Oh yes, theories…' He paused and frowned, as if marshalling his thoughts. 'What's the deal with Professor Shulough and you, then?'

Kendle's face hardened. 'What are you suggesting?'

he whispered menacingly.

The Doctor took a step back and waved his hands airily, demonstrating both that he meant no harm and, more importantly, that he wasn't armed. He wished he'd had the foresight to put his glasses on – a man like Kendle would never hit a chap wearing glasses, would he?

'I was just wondering, that's all. How the pair of you hooked up. Why you're so loyal to her. That's all. Nothing else.'

Whatever offence Kendle had taken, he seemed prepared to accept this as an apology. He sat back down in his seat. 'She's my niece,' he told the Doctor.

'You're her uncle!' the Doctor said, genuinely caught out by this revelation.

'That's how it usually works. She's my late sister's daughter.'

'An uncle, the uncle,' repeated the Doctor, running the new information through his head like a computer accepting new data. 'Uncle Kendle the Marine. Right… You said your sister was dead?'

Kendle bowed his head.

'Petra was just ten when it happened. My sister and brother-in-law were members of Guillan's crew. She saw them leave on board the *Armstrong* and they came back in coffins.'

The Doctor nodded. It was all beginning to make sense now.

'It was just one of those terrible things. I was away,

fighting in the war. I came back and took Petra in.'

'You brought her up?'

'She was my sister's only child,' he replied simply, as if that said everything, and in a way it did.

'You must be proud of her. She seems to have turned out really well, all things considered,' the Doctor said after a pause.

Kendle raised his head and looked the Doctor squarely in the eyes. 'Do you really think so?'

The Doctor hesitated, for once choosing not to fill a silence with a stream of words.

'She used to be a jolly little girl,' continued Kendle. 'Always laughing.'

He got up and made himself busy at another console. Even though Kendle's back was turned, the Doctor could tell he was tearful at the memory.

'I don't think I've seen her laugh since her parents died.'

'Grief can be a terrible thing,' the Doctor suggested sympathetically.

Kendle spun round to face the Doctor. 'But it has to end some time. You have to move on.'

'And she hasn't?'

Kendle sat back against the console. 'I just don't know. She doesn't ever talk about it. She's so driven. First it was to complete her schooling. Then it was to get every higher academic qualification she could. And finally she began researching space lore, all the myths and legends of the last frontier.'

'All of which eventually brought her here. To paradise.'

Kendle nodded. 'But do you think it will make her happy?' He then shook his head sadly before answering his own question. 'I myself rather doubt it…'

The Doctor decided it was only fair to leave the man alone with his private thoughts. But as he went to see how the others were getting on, he had a lot of new information to mull over.

In the lab Hespell and Baker were already engaged in the business of producing a sufficient quantity of the jinnen mixture. Rez was watching, fascinated, but Kaylen was wandering round the lab, looking very uncomfortable, like a trapped animal.

'How are you doing?' asked the Doctor, as he strode in.

'Not long now,' Hespell reported.

A large tank had been filled with brown liquid, which was bubbling away furiously. It resembled alchemy more than science, but the Doctor smiled his approval regardless. He then turned his attention to Kaylen, who was still looking at everything with a mixture of fear and apprehension.

'All a bit much for you?' he asked. 'All this…' He waved an arm around the room, but his gesture took in the entire spaceship.

Kaylen nodded, grateful for his understanding.

'I think I'll get back to the village,' she suggested nervously.

The Doctor frowned. 'It's getting dark out there.'

Kaylen gave him a shy shrug. 'I know my way through the forest. I know where the traps are.'

'Traps?' queried the Doctor. 'What traps?'

Rose was finding it increasingly difficult to see where she was treading. The canopy of leaves, coupled with the setting sun, meant that it was getting very dark at ground level and she kept tripping over raised roots.

Even the professor, who was by now very hot and sweaty, had agreed to slow down, fearing that their headlong pace might give them both twisted ankles. 'How far away are these ruins, then?' she demanded.

Rose wasn't sure she could answer with any authority. She had a mental picture of the relative positions of the village, the spaceship and the ruined city, and in her head at least they were equidistant, about five kilometres apart. She couldn't be certain, but she imagined that they'd been walking for well over an hour by now. Surely that was long enough to cover five kilometres?

'It can't be far now,' she said, but the professor didn't looked very convinced.

A nearby tree had low-slung branches that offered an easy climb and, to Rose's surprise, the older woman suddenly grabbed one and started up the tree.

'What are you doing?' Rose cried in surprise.

The professor, showing skills that would flatter a monkey, was already disappearing into the higher reaches. She was now high enough to push her head through the top branches and look out over the rest of the forest.

'I'm getting our bearings, of course,' she replied. 'And I can see something, some kind of tower.'

'That'll be the central temple, then,' Rose told her.

As quickly as she had climbed the tree, the professor descended. 'It's over that way,' she said, with a 'told you so' look. She was pointing away from the path.

'The Laylorans said to keep to the path,' Rose reminded her.

'The shortest way between two points is a straight line,' replied the professor. 'This path may be a lot of things, but it isn't straight.'

Without waiting for any further discussion, she set off in the direction she had indicated. Rose had no choice but to follow her.

Two minutes later disaster struck. It happened very quickly: one moment the professor had been walking along in front of her and the next she was gone. The ground seemed to collapse under her feet. Rose realised that what had appeared to be a solid carpet of leaves and undergrowth was, in fact, just a thin covering that concealed a deep pit.

Rose crept closer to the edge and peered into the darkness. 'Are you all right?' she called down, unable to make out anything in the gloom.

'Just the odd bruise,' the professor's voice floated up from the blackness. 'No major damage. Apart from to my pride, of course.'

It was the nearest thing to a joke that Rose had ever heard from the professor. The woman must be in shock, she thought, a little unkindly.

Now that her eyes were adjusting to the light, Rose could make out the figure of the professor, sitting on the floor of the pit some four metres below. It was a long drop but some of the matting that had concealed the pit had fallen with her and cushioned the impact.

'I'll try and find something to get you out,' Rose said, but the professor just shook her head in response.

'Go back to the ship. Get help from there,' she instructed, but it was too late. Rose had already moved away.

The sun had all but disappeared now, making it hard to discern very much at all. Rose saw that several of the plants round about resembled vines; perhaps she could make some kind of rope? Taking care not to fall into any traps herself, she began to collect suitable vines, winding them round her arm like a garden hose. She was about to head back in the direction of the pit and the professor when, from somewhere nearby, a twig cracked and she could hear rustling in the undergrowth.

Rose froze where she was, hardly daring to breathe, her left leg hovering a few centimetres above the ground. Was she hearing the professor moving deep in the pit? She couldn't be certain. It had sounded closer than that, hadn't it? Slowly, she placed her foot down and, having regained her balance, she tried to see where the noise was coming from. There it was, over to her left. Something was clearly progressing through the forest. Dare she call out, or would that be a mistake? A moment later she knew that staying quiet had been the right strategy, as a Witiku appeared, pushing through the trees. Had it seen her?

'Rose? Rose, are you there?'

The Witiku stopped at the sound of the human voice and changed direction, moving away from Rose and back towards the pit. Rose followed it, going as quickly as she could but making sure she did nothing to draw attention to herself.

The Witiku was roaring now, sensing prey.

'Rose?'

This time there was no doubting the fear in the woman's voice. She was trapped and the monster was about to find her, cornered and vulnerable. Rose couldn't ignore her.

'Professor, it's one of the creatures,' she called out desperately. 'Look, I've found something we can use as rope, but you'll have to be ready when I say the word!'

Unfortunately, shouting like this meant the creature was now aware of a second human to target. It swung round and faced Rose, who realised that the pit was between her and the Witiku. Moving quickly, she tied one end of her vine 'rope' round a thick tree trunk at the side of the pit. She looked up from completing her knot to see where the monster had got to. It was circling the pit in a clockwise direction. Leaving the vine, Rose started moving in the same direction.

The Witiku extended its terrifying talons with a noise like knives being sharpened. If it wasn't for the danger she was in, Rose thought, the scene might look quite amusing. The Savage Beast and the Plucky Heroine, dancing round the Pit of Death!

She realised she was now back at the place where she'd tied the vine. Not taking her eyes off the monster, she crouched down and tipped the untied end of the rope into the pit.

'Grab hold now,' she instructed the professor. 'But don't start climbing yet!'

Watching the Witiku getting ever closer, Rose knew what she had to do. The creatures were big and heavy, but that was also a weakness. They weren't exactly nimble. She'd have to time this to perfection, but they had no other choice. She could now smell the familiar odour of the creature's fur and could hear its ragged and angry breathing. It raised one of its upper arms, ready to slice down at her.

Now, she thought, and dived towards the creature's legs, rolling under its arms and pulling off a credible forward roll. Getting to her feet as quickly as she could, she saw that the Witiku had also turned around. Roaring angrily, it took another step towards her.

Again, she had to make sure her timing was impeccable. She dropped her shoulder and charged at the creature's legs. Mickey had once given her a long lecture about the art of the rugby tackle. It had been pretty tedious at the time, but she had remembered one key idea – hit hard and hit low. She shoulder-barged the Witiku just below its knee with her full weight. She twisted and rolled to one side, praying that the talons arcing through the air wouldn't connect. Above her, the creature flailed its arms, its whole body knocked off balance. For a moment it seemed to be frozen in midair, and then, finally, it fell backwards into the trap, roaring angrily the whole way down.

Rose got to her feet quickly and ran to the edge of the pit, screaming, 'Professor! Climb now, Professor!'

At the bottom of the pit she could just make out the thrashing figure of the Witiku, but much closer another figure was moving. Climbing up the side of the pit, using the vine, was the professor.

She was surprisingly agile for an older woman, Rose thought. A moment later a hand popped up and Rose grabbed it. As the professor clambered out of the pit she was breathing heavily and looked a little pale, but she was otherwise unharmed. They could hear that back down in the pit the creature was getting to its feet and attempting to climb out after them.

'Come on,' urged Rose, who was still holding the older woman's hand.

They began to run in the direction of the ruins. Rose

just hoped there were no more traps along the way. The professor, who seemed to be in a state of shock, had never appeared more human to Rose before.

'Why did you come back for me?' she gasped.

'Couldn't leave you down there, could I?' Rose replied, without slowing down.

'But you could have been hurt. Or worse. You should have left me.'

Rose slowed down. They'd reached the more complete buildings now and the temple, which was their target, was in sight. Just another hundred metres or so. But Rose was tiring, and if the frantic running was getting to her, what was it doing to the professor? The pair of them stopped and both bent double, trying desperately to control their breathing. Rose glanced over at the professor and shook her head.

'I couldn't just leave you. We don't do things like that.'

For a moment the professor wondered who the 'we' was, but then she realised. 'You and the Doctor?' she asked, and Rose nodded a confirmation. 'So what kind of things do you do? Rescue people, fight monsters?'

'Yeah, that's about the size of it,' Rose confirmed. 'That and run a lot! Come on!'

The Witiku that had fallen into the pit burst out of the forest some distance behind them. It was going to be a foot race now. Rose and the professor set off, the younger woman leading the way towards the entrance.

They were now running along the side wall of the temple. Suddenly she became aware of movement over to her left. A glance confirmed her worst fears. Three more of the creatures were moving to cut them off.

'Rose!' called the professor with alarm. 'There are more of them!'

Rose was about to say that she had already seen them when she realised that the professor was looking in another direction entirely.

Rose spun around, frantically looking for an escape route, but there wasn't one. They had nowhere left to run. The creatures had them surrounded.

TWELVE

Kendle found the Doctor in the professor's quarters, looking through her precious collection of Paradise Planet evidence. He knew he ought to be angry, but the expression on the stranger's face pulled him up short. It was identical to the one he'd seen on his niece's face a thousand times before. A look of puzzled concentration, as if at any moment a vital connection would be made.

The Doctor didn't look up from the journal he was reading even though he must have heard Kendle enter the room.

'The answer is in all this somewhere,' he said, as if that explained everything.

'You shouldn't be in here,' Kendle started, but then changed tack as what the Doctor had said registered. 'What answer? What's the question?'

The Doctor glanced over his shoulder and raised his eyebrows behind his glasses. 'Ah, that's just it. If I knew the question I'd be halfway there. Thing is, I don't know the question or the answer. Which makes looking for either really, really difficult.' He turned away modestly and grinned. 'Still, wouldn't want it to be too easy, would we? Where's the fun in that?'

'I don't understand,' replied Kendle.

'Are you going to stand there feeding me straight lines all night or are you going to try and help?'

The ex-marine's training came to the fore. Intelligence gathering. Specify target. Focus on the key data.

'What do we know about the planet?' asked the Doctor.

'That it's meant to be a paradise,' replied Kendle.

'But why do we think that?'

Kendle nodded at the direction of the journal. 'Because Guillan came here and described it.'

The Doctor nodded and flicked through a few more pages.

'He certainly did – in great detail. Reckoned himself a bit of a poet, did old Guillan. Shame he wasn't. It's like reading *Hamlet* before my final edit... Now, the thing he keeps going on about is balance.'

'Balance?'

The Doctor pointed out a few paragraphs on the page he had reached.

'Here – "every element of the ecosystem is in balance", you see... and then he goes on to list in what ways. I think your man Guillan was a bit of a tree-hugger. All this yin and yang stuff going on.'

'So what are you saying? That those creatures are part of this balance? That every now and again the locals start turning into monsters and it's all part of the cycle of nature on this planet?' Kendle didn't sound at all convinced.

The Doctor shook his head. 'No, I'm not saying that at all. It doesn't fit. There's something else.' He flipped further into the journal, scanning the pages at incredible speed, until he reached the end. 'Hang on… what's this…' he muttered, reading the final entry again.

Kendle came closer to look over the Doctor's shoulder.

And now we must leave this heavenly paradise, and take away with us our human and ancient imperfections. Faced with such beauty we have no choice but to accept our uncleanliness and return to the harsh realities of our own filthy lives.

'I see what you mean about the poetry. It's a bit over the top, isn't it?' Kendle said.

To his surprise, however, the Doctor didn't agree. Instead, he slammed shut the journal and pulled his glasses from his face. 'Yes!' he announced, eyes wide with delight. 'That's it!'

'What is?' demanded Kendle, confused.

The Doctor started talking very fast and Kendle had to strain to keep up.

'It's not a metaphor at all. He's being factual, you know, not poetic. The planet's got a perfectly balanced ecosystem, right? So what happens if you add a new element to something that's perfectly balanced? You send it out of kilter. And what are we here? Alien. We're the new element. We're making the planet ill and the Witiku are the planet's response. It's as if the planet itself is allergic to us!' He stopped and looked serious. 'We have to sort this out – fast – before the entire planet suffers a fatal anaphylactic shock. And that is a metaphor,' he added, 'for the end of the world!'

Rose ran through the options. To her right – monsters. To her left – monsters. In front of her – monsters. Just another day at the office, then. No possibilities up or down, so the only way to go was backwards, but that was just a solid wall. No convenient entrance there. Bad planning.

Beside her Petra Shulough was shaking with fear. She grabbed the older woman's hand and gave it a squeeze. With her other hand, she felt the uneven surface of the wall at their backs. It was rough and uneven; the individual stones were not all the same size and some jutted out slightly. Maybe up was an option after all. There was a window set in the wall about three metres from the ground – could she reach it? It was certainly worth a try.

'Quick! Help me up,' she hissed at Petra.

Petra put her hands together and Rose placed her foot into them, then pushed off. She scrabbled for a handhold with her left hand – and found one. Moving quickly but carefully, she found a secure place for her left foot and then her right. She was clinging to the wall, Spider-Man fashion, but without the dodgy skin-tight costume. Not far to go now. She stretched up with her right arm and felt for the window ledge. Got it.

With a huge and unladylike grunt Rose hauled herself up and over the ledge, into the room on the other side. From there she was able to reach down to help the professor, who was already starting her own ascent. And with good reason – the nearest Witiku was only a few metres away.

Rose clasped the professor's arms and pulled with all her strength. The older woman was quite light, thankfully, and a moment or two later she was through the window. Below, an enraged Witiku had arrived at the base of the wall and was trying to slice at them. Its talons raked the stone just below the ledge, causing sparks to fly. The two women exchanged looks and smiled, then Rose led the way deeper into the building.

'Thank you,' gasped the professor as they went. 'That's twice you've saved my life.'

'There are worse habits,' joked Rose as they reached a stone spiral staircase.

They could hear the roars of the creatures all around them, but it was impossible to work out how close they were.

'Up or down?' Rose wondered aloud, trying to work out the lie of the land.

She knew this was the main temple building that she had partly explored earlier. Up would take them to side galleries and then on to the observation tower that the Doctor had climbed. From there they would be able to see their attackers coming but they would also be trapped. Down would lead to the crypt. Although the cellars and tunnels there were dark and dangerous, they had the advantage of being extensive. With luck they would be able to lose their pursuers that way. Rose had made up her mind.

'Down?' queried the professor, following her.

'You wanted to see the crystals, didn't you?' Rose smiled encouragingly, and led the way down the spiral staircase.

Kendle regarded his troops with a critical eye. Not the finest body of soldiers that he had ever commanded but they would have to do. Hespell, the red-headed trainee pilot, looked paler than ever, and his female colleague, Baker, didn't look much better. The pair of them had graduated from the Space Naval Academy just before he had taken them on and, from the records he had seen, neither of them had excelled at the combat-training element of their course. The third member of his assault squad was the human turned native – Rez. He seemed calmer than the other two, even though they were at least eight years older than him. Perhaps it was the advantage of knowing the territory.

The final member of the team was the Doctor and Kendle just didn't know where to begin with this one. He didn't look like a fighter – tall and thin, you could imagine him snapping in two like a twig in the hands of a Witiku. Yet there was an inner strength to him, a steel core, well hidden but definitely there, that even Kendle found intimidating.

The belts they each wore, from which numerous plastic bags hung, did not improve the impression of a makeshift army about to face the enemy with no weapons. Each bag was filled with the solution the Doctor had designed, and the sophisticated, high-tech delivery system for this bio-weapon was to be the human arm. In short, they were going to lob the bags at the creatures, like kids in a summer garden hurling water balloons at each other. Kendle grimaced and was glad none of the professional soldiers he had led into countless battles could see him now. In addition to the jinnera 'bombs', each of them carried a makeshift water pistol, a hose connected to a pump-action container of liquid.

Kendle sighed to himself. 'All right, let's move out. Rez, you know the territory, you take point.'

The young human looked confused at the order.

'Lead the way,' the Doctor explained kindly.

Rez nodded and set off. Hespell and Baker fell in behind him. The Doctor hesitated but Kendle waved him on, taking up the final position in the formation.

Outside the spaceship, the forest was now dark.

Dark but not silent. Animal noises filled the air, together with the calls and hoots of nocturnal birds. As they followed the teenager into the darkness, Hespell and Baker looked around nervously. Without a word, Hespell found himself reaching out and taking his colleague's hand. She returned the quick squeeze and they continued forward together, still holding hands.

Behind them both the Doctor and Kendle saw this unorthodox military manoeuvre. Kendle sighed, audibly this time. The Doctor just smiled. How human, he thought. And then the smile faded as he remembered Rose. He was sure she'd be OK. In all their adventures she had proved herself a worthy companion time and time again; nevertheless, he admitted to himself, he would feel a lot happier when they were reunited once more.

Rose reckoned they had Brother Hugan to thank for the illumination. It was because of his devotion to the old ways that the temple building was still in use – if only largely for storage – and that meant a number of torches had been left at various strategic points, together with flint and fuel. Rose had found one, fixed into a metal holder, as they had reached the bottom of the spiral staircase. She had carefully removed it and now it was at least giving them a fighting chance of seeing what they were doing. Not that Rose actually knew where any of the passages led, but at least they could see the uneven floor at their feet.

They had been walking in silence for some time now, going ever deeper into the labyrinth of storerooms and connecting corridors. They'd seen stores of dried fruit, cloth and jinnen powder and more rooms like the one Rose had seen before, full of crystals, but the professor's curiosity had been muted. Right now she was more interested in survival than in the state of her ship's engines.

'Do you think we're safe yet?' she asked, in a voice devoid of her usual arrogance and authority.

Rose was amused at the way she had somehow become the leader of their little expedition. She considered her answer for a moment. The sound of the creatures' cries had faded, but that could just mean that they were no longer roaring, not that they were far away.

'I don't know,' she answered eventually, 'but I think we should keep moving.'

They had reached an archway into another large chamber. Rose raised the torch above her head, to cast the light as widely as possible. There was a shape over to her left, massive and inhuman. Rose gasped and was about to run when she realised there were more of them. Five or six in total, all around the edge of the room – Witiku. Had they walked into a trap?

Then, with relief, Rose saw that these Witiku were statues – huge stone replicas of the creatures that were chasing them. In the centre of the room was a vast slab of stone – like the sacrificial altar in the main temple above but on a much larger scale. Rose swallowed. This altar stone was stained too, with a deep black mark. Whatever had been sacrificed here was a lot larger than a bird or a hog.

Rose glanced at the professor, who was regarding the stone with academic interest. She caught Rose's eye and Rose could see that they had both reached the same conclusion about the function of this altar. This chamber was a real killing pit – a place where the ancient Laylorans had practised human sacrifice. The two women looked at each other and nodded – they were not going to stay here a moment longer than necessary.

At the far end of the chamber there was another archway to yet another corridor. They hurried towards it, but as they moved away, carrying the only light, something stirred behind one of the Witiku statues. Cold, hard eyes watched the flame disappear into the darkness. Then something began to follow, moving with panther-like stealth.

The Doctor had joined Rez at the head of their group. He was glad of his large coat but the human boy seemed immune to the cold night. Hardened to the local conditions, the Doctor supposed. Rez had obviously adapted to the planet's climate. But had the planet adapted to having him here?

It appeared that he had been harbouring similar

thoughts. 'You think the Witiku have risen because the spaceship crashed here?' he asked the Doctor.

'I think the mass production of Witiku is a response to the professor's ship, yes…' the Doctor began, but it was clear to the boy that this wasn't a full answer.

'But the first Witiku appeared before the ship came down?' continued Rez.

'Yes,' nodded the Doctor solemnly.

'So they were a reaction to a different problem. Like all the other things. The crop failures. The strange weather. The earth tremors.'

The Doctor was fascinated. 'And these things are unusual for Laylora?'

'Very. The elders told me that nothing like this has happened before. But it's been getting worse year by year now. And no one understands why.'

'But you think you do, don't you?' He let the question hang in the air for a moment. 'How long has this been going on?' he asked, fearing that he already knew what the reply would be.

'Fifteen years,' Rez told him sadly. 'Since they found me,' he added in a small voice.

They walked on in silence.

A few minutes later Kendle's unit reached the outlying ruins. Here, where the tree cover was less dense, Laylora's twin moons bathed the area in an eerie bluish light, making the landscape look stranger than ever before. It was very cold now too, and their breath misted in front of their faces. The five of them stood together for a moment, regarding the mysterious scene before them.

'Now where?' asked Kendle.

The Doctor shrugged. 'Not sure. Why don't we head for the main temple? I bet that's where we'll find the monsters,' he suggested. 'To be honest, I was rather expecting to have been attacked by now!'

Rose stopped suddenly and the professor cannoned into her.

'Witiku,' whispered Rose, turning around on the spot. 'We need to go back the way we came.'

The professor turned and took the lead, but she had only gone a short distance when she too came to an abrupt stop. Something was moving in the darkness. Rose still had the torch, so she couldn't see very well, but something was definitely up ahead.

'There's something in front of us too,' she whispered to Rose. 'Now what?'

Rose looked around quickly. There was a chamber entrance a metre or so away, but it was likely to have only the one entrance – if they sheltered in there they would be trapped. A roar from behind made the decision for her and she pulled the older woman into the chamber. They'd just have to hope the Doctor was on his way.

The attack party had already suffered a few setbacks.

The terrain was treacherous and they had all stumbled and slipped as they hurried towards the temple building. Unfortunately, their falls had come at a price. Both Hespell and Baker had lost some of their jinnera bombs. Indeed, Hespell had a soaking-wet leg where a brace of bags had burst prematurely. Nevertheless, they had reached the temple without any serious injury and with most of their precious cargo intact.

The Doctor led the way into the dark interior. Moving quickly, they found a couple of torches. The Doctor took one, giving the other to Baker, and he then led the way down the stone steps into the crypt. They could hear Witiku activity up ahead. Each of them now had one of the jinnera bombs to hand, ready to throw.

'Aim at the body,' instructed the Doctor. 'The bags will break on impact and we should get maximum coverage that way.'

'And you're sure that will cure them?' Hespell gave voice to the question they all wanted to ask.

'Well, nothing in life's ever certain,' the Doctor replied. 'Except death and taxes – and neither of them has ever troubled me!'

They had now reached a passageway and were moving towards sounds of activity. Witiku roaring – loud and angry – floated back to them.

'Stand by,' muttered the Doctor. 'Sounds like we've found them.'

He scouted on ahead, poking his head round the

edge of an arched doorway. His eyes quickly adjusted to the light and he was able to see what was happening. Six or seven Witiku were in front of him, facing into a room containing a huge pile of yellow crystals. And on the top of the pile perched Rose and the professor.

Rose was hurling crystals at the creatures to keep them at bay. The Doctor stepped back into the corridor and signalled for the others to join him.

'Half a dozen of them,' he reported, 'just inside the door. Are you ready?'

Kendle and Rez nodded immediately; Hespell and Baker gave each other a reassuring look first.

'Right, then – let's do it,' said the Doctor.

The five of them quickly lined up across the doorway.

'Oi, you lot – over here!' cried the Doctor, and the Witiku spun round to face him. 'Now!' he ordered, hurling his first jinnera bomb at the nearest creature.

The others did the same. Five bags of the solution sailed through the air and all hit their targets. As promised, the bags broke on impact, spraying their victims with the liquid. Each of the Witiku screamed as if on fire.

'Quickly! Another one!' shouted the Doctor.

A second volley flew through the air and again the Witiku screamed as the liquid burned their hairy skins, but still they kept moving forward. There was no sign of any transformation. The only result was that now the Witiku were wet and angry and heading directly for the rescue party, talons raised, ready to strike.

Something had gone very wrong.

THIRTEEN

Ironically it was Rose and the professor who came to the Doctor's rescue. A new hail of trisilicate rained down on the maddened creatures, causing them to turn their attention again to their initial targets. In the confusion, Rez pulled Hespell and Baker back into the corridor.

The Doctor and Kendle, however, both had concerns for the women on top of the crystal mountain. Kendle dived to the left and the Doctor went to the right, but both had the same thought in mind. They ran, fast and low, around the line of creatures and scrambled up each side of the pile of trisilicate. At the top, the professor and Rose kept up their attack, distracting the creatures by lobbing the heaviest crystals at them, preventing them from getting to either the Doctor or Kendle.

Climbing the pile wasn't easy. The stones kept shifting beneath their feet and offered precious little in the way of secure handholds either. The Doctor was reminded of trying to run on the shingle beach at Brighton. Keeping his flaming torch held high further complicated the climb. Nevertheless, with the roars of the angry Witiku urging them on, the Doctor and Kendle reached the summit, where they joined Rose and the professor in their rock-throwing assault.

'Nice to see ya,' said a smiling Rose.

'You too.' The Doctor grinned back at her.

'So, you got anything else apart from water bombs? Maybe a catapult or something? Or are you going to try flicking ink at them?' Rose asked, with more than a hint of sarcasm.

'That was jinnera in a solution. It was meant to reverse the transformation,' explained the Doctor.

'Didn't work,' said Rose flatly.

'Yeah, I noticed that.'

The Witiku were still trying to reach them, so Rose picked up a fresh handful of crystals and continued to lob them at the creatures. Out of the corner of her eye she could see the Doctor starting to fiddle with the nozzle of a container slung around his neck, pulling out the short hose attached to a spray control.

'Maybe we just need a bigger dose,' he speculated, and let loose with a shower of the solution.

Rose watched as the liquid shot out under pressure and poured down over the nearest creatures, but it proved no more effective than the bombs had been.

Kendle had now joined the women in hurling the largest lumps of trisilicate they could find at the creatures. Despite their best efforts, however, the Witiku were beginning to get much higher up the crystal mountain.

'Perhaps the others will get help?' Rose suggested.

The Doctor was looking around, desperately.

'Hang about,' he said. 'How did these crystals get here?'

'The locals collect them,' the professor answered.

'They find them in their fields,' added Rose

'Yeah, yeah, I know that, but how do they get *here*? In a pile like this? They're not going to come through that door with a wheelbarrow full and lob them up here, are they? For one thing, they don't have wheelbarrows…'

Rose realised what he was saying. 'You mean, it's like a coal cellar?'

Mickey's gran used to live in an old terraced council house which had a coal cellar. Rose remembered Mickey telling her how he used to play in it until one day he got locked in by mistake and had never gone near the place again. If this trisilicate store operated the same way there must be –

'A trapdoor!' announced the Doctor, delighted.

He was holding the flaming torch high in the air. The ceiling to the room was about two metres away from where they were precariously balanced on the trisilicate mountain and directly above them they could see a wooden trapdoor.

'Shall I give you a leg-up?' suggested the Doctor,

passing his torch to the professor and then holding his hands together.

Rose planted her foot and pushed up, then swung her legs round to sit on the Doctor's shoulders. Now her head was pushing against the trapdoor. She positioned her hands on the panel and shoved. It was stiff and heavy but she could feel it gradually succumbing to the pressure. She tried again, wincing with the effort. The roars of the Witiku were getting closer. With a final burst of strength, Rose thrust her arms up and the trapdoor gave way. The twin doors moved apart and fell away to the sides. Rose then quickly scrambled up into the room above. The Doctor passed her a torch and then helped the professor to follow Rose to safety.

Rose helped the professor to her feet and gave her the torch to hold. As the professor backed away from the hatch to make room for the Doctor and Kendle, something suddenly snatched it from her grasp. Sharp talons curled around her neck. Another Witiku? But this one seemed smaller than the others. A voice close to her ear confirmed that this was no ordinary Witiku.

'Close the hatch,' it ordered in a husky growl.

Rose whirled round in surprise.

To her horror she saw that it was Brother Hugan. He was inside the Witiku costume that Rez had been wearing when she first met him. More importantly, he was holding the professor hostage.

'Close the hatch,' he repeated, 'or she dies here.'

'Rose?' It was the Doctor's voice floating up from below. 'Is there a problem?'

Rose couldn't take her eyes away from Brother Hugan. He made to rake the talons across the petrified professor's neck. The threat was clear. She really had no choice.

With a lump in her throat, Rose flipped the twin doors shut again, trapping the Doctor and Kendle with the monsters and leaving herself at the mercy of the madman. Things surely couldn't get any worse!

Without any torches, Hespell and Baker were literally running in the dark. They had stumbled and fallen more than once and had been forced to slow the pace of their escape. Rez, who knew the terrain best, was leading the way, but he kept having to slow down to allow the other two to catch up. Still, at least they could not hear any sounds of pursuit behind them. It seemed that the creatures were more interested in the humans trapped in the trisilicate store than in them.

'But we can't just leave them,' gasped Baker, as she stopped to catch her breath.

Hespell came to a halt too and looked at his colleague. His eyes were adjusting to the scant light now and he could see the conflicting emotions on her face. They both felt the same way: guilty about fleeing and yet scared to do anything to help.

'I know – but what can we do?' he replied.

Rez came back to find them.

'We need to keep moving,' he told them.

'Ssh!' Baker said suddenly. 'I think I heard something.'

Rez looked around, startled. She was right. There were sounds coming from further down the corridor ahead of them. Were they trapped between two separate groups of Witiku?

Hespell took Baker's hand again and pulled her close, so he could put a protective arm around her. Rez moved ahead, towards the sounds. A light was now clearly visible, moving towards them.

'Hello?' Rez called out nervously.

Figures appeared in the gloom, but they were not Witiku. It was a group of the natives, led by Mother Jaelette and Kaylen.

The younger Layloran rushed to hug her adopted brother. Embarrassed, Rez detached himself.

'The Witiku have the Doctor and the others trapped in the crystal store,' he told them urgently. 'The Doctor's jinnera solution didn't work.'

Jaelette nodded, grim-faced. 'The idea was good but the dose is not strong enough,' she told them. She raised her hand and showed them that she was holding a sharpened section of jinnen bush. 'Maybe this will be more effective.'

Hespell and Baker had been listening intently.

'Have you any spares?' asked Hespell, indicating the homemade weapon.

'Plenty,' answered Jaelette. 'When Kaylen came back and told us the Doctor's plan, I thought about all the stories Brother Hugan has told us about our history. And I also thought about how we kill the animals in the killing pits. We use this traditional wooden spear, which is called a witona – it means "talon of the Witiku". You see, we coat the spear in the thickest jinnen bean paste.' She showed them the dark points of the weapons.

She then nodded at the dozen or so Laylorans with her and a couple of the witona spears were produced for Baker and Hespell. The new weapons were about half a metre in length, long enough to throw or jab at the enemy, though not without risk.

'You would have to get very close to use these,' commented Rez, as he took a weapon for himself.

'Then we shall just have to be careful,' Jaelette said firmly, and headed towards the fight.

The Doctor and Kendle were back to back on the summit of the trisilicate mountain, surrounded on all sides by Witiku. The creatures were getting closer with every passing second. Kendle produced a laser weapon from a holster.

'No!' ordered the Doctor firmly. 'No energy weapons. We mustn't forget that these are all innocent Laylorans.'

Kendle regarded the approaching creatures, which were swinging their talons in front of them as they came. 'They're not going to cut us any slack, though, are they?' He raised his weapon again.

'I said no!' the Doctor repeated angrily.

'And I heard you. I'll fire at their feet, try and dislodge them. OK?'

Without waiting for an answer, Kendle did exactly as he had said. Shooting just beneath the feet of the nearest Witiku, he blasted a sizeable hole in the uneven surface of the crystal mountain. The Witiku overbalanced and toppled backwards, taking two of its fellows down at the same time. The trio tumbled over and over, roaring furiously.

'Nice shooting,' the Doctor commented.

'Thank you,' Kendle responded, swinging round to try the same trick on the other side.

The Doctor's eyes were caught by some activity near the doorway. 'Look,' he cried, pointing.

There was a blaze of light as fresh torches came into the chamber, illuminating the Layloran counter-attack. Hespell and Baker led the charge, heading straight for the trio of Witiku still getting to their feet. They hurled their spears into the nearest two and then backed off to allow Mother Jaelette, who was hard on their heels, to hit the third. On the other side of the room, Kaylen and the other Laylorans attacked the Witiku that were still climbing.

'It's the cavalry,' grinned the Doctor.

To his delight, the two creatures attacked by Hespell and Baker were already shaking, convulsing and beginning to transform, exactly like Brother Hugan had in the spaceship hold.

The rest of the Laylorans flooded into the chamber, firing their spears at the remaining Witiku. The creatures all fell quickly, shuddering, and began to change shape. In just a few moments of action the situation had been completely turned around. Instead of a crowd of angry creatures there were numerous dazed and naked Laylorans lying all over the room. Mother Jaelette had come prepared, however, and a number of her party were carrying blankets, clothes and moccasins. Others had water and dressings to deal with the flesh wounds made by the spears.

The immediate danger over, the Doctor and Kendle clambered down to the floor of the chamber and joined the rescue party. Among the recovering Laylorans, who had recently been Witiku, were the missing Aerack, Serenta and Purin. All three were very pale and shaken, having spent longest in the transformed state. As soon as the victims were able to walk the other Laylorans began taking them back up to the surface.

Mother Jaelette came over to join the Doctor and the humans. They watched together as the Layloran rescue party and the recovering ex-Witiku filed out of the chamber.

'Thank you,' the Doctor said simply.

'It was your idea,' replied Jaelette. 'We just improved on the delivery method.'

'Well, I'm glad you did.' The Doctor glanced around. 'Have we accounted for everyone who was missing?'

'Everyone except Brother Hugan,' Jaelette told him.

The Doctor looked suddenly alarmed. 'Rose and the professor!'

Kendle knew immediately what the Doctor was thinking.

'What is the room above this chamber?' he demanded of the native woman.

Jaelette thought for a moment, working her way through a mental map of the cellars.

'The Hall of Offering,' she announced finally.

'What kind of offering?' asked the Doctor darkly, not liking the sound of that at all.

'It was used in the dark times,' Jaelette explained, looking embarrassed. 'Our ancestors were... more primitive. They used to believe that it was necessary to make sacrifices to Laylora.'

'Sacrifices? What kind of sacrifices?'

Mother Jaelette looked away, unable to meet his gaze.

'People,' she said in a quiet voice. 'They used to sacrifice people.'

Professor Shulough was utterly helpless. The madman had made Rose tie her hands and her feet. The girl had done her best to make the knots as loose as possible, but the professor was no escapologist. She had been left lying on the cold stone floor at the foot of one of the giant statues that lined the ceremonial chamber they were now in.

Rose, meanwhile, was lying on the large stone altar in the centre of the room. The Layloran shaman had used a pad soaked in jinnera to knock the poor girl out and for the last few minutes the professor had seen little sign of life from her. Perhaps this was a kindness. Brother Hugan had produced a vicious-looking curved knife, which he had offered up to the various statues for approval. The professor had winced, fearing that he was going to plunge it into Rose's heart without any further delay, but instead he had placed the sacrificial knife by her side and started to intone a chant.

She realised, with some relief, that this was a ceremony with a very strict running order. The act of sacrifice would be the climax. Before then, the shaman would have to go through a number of ritual acts. With luck it would give her the time she needed. She began to wrestle with her bonds anew, encouraged by the slight give she could feel in the knots.

The shaman was now performing some kind of dance, crying out like a wild animal as he flailed his arms around. The talons on his costume scythed through the air above Rose's prone body.

Suddenly the professor was aware of a new arrival. Out of the corner of her eye she had the impression of a familiar dark-suited figure striding confidently into the room.

'Hey, old fella,' shouted the Doctor, coming to a halt. 'I want a word with you.'

The shaman stopped his chant and reached for the knife.

'Hold it right there,' ordered the Doctor, in such a commanding voice that the costumed Brother Hugan found himself obeying.

'Laylora must be appeased,' the Layloran insisted, his voice cracking with emotion.

His eyes were wild, the Doctor noted. Clearly the strain of recent events had pushed him over the edge.

'Laylora doesn't need you to kill anyone,' the Doctor began, in a more considered tone.

The shaman shook his head. 'She is angry. Only the blood of an outsider will appease her.'

'You reckon?'

The Doctor was moving now, pacing back and forth, hands thrust deep into his pockets. The shaman's head followed the movement, like a spectator at Wimbledon, one way and then the other, almost hypnotised.

'Because I don't. Thing is, you see,' the Doctor continued, suddenly stopping his pacing and pointing at the shaman, 'you've almost got it right.' He waved an arm around, taking in the chamber, the temple, the whole planet. 'Laylora *is* like a living creature. This place, this planet, it's perfect... everything in balance, everything. Only the trouble is, it's too perfect. Stick something in this system that doesn't belong here and all hell's let loose.'

Behind the Doctor, at the entrance to the hall, Kendle, Baker, Rez and some of the other Laylorans entered slowly, but held back to allow the Doctor to remain the focus of the shaman's attention. The Doctor, although aware of them, didn't look round. He concentrated on Brother Hugan and continued to speak.

'Laylora doesn't need a sacrifice. She doesn't need "appeasing". She needs relief. She's suffering an allergic reaction – to us outsiders. You remember when the humans came before? Fifty years ago? Mr Guillan and his people? They worked it out. They saw it happen. Their presence here caused the same reaction.'

The Doctor could see that he was getting close now. The shaman was listening to him.

'If we all just leave, everything will go back to normal,' he promised Brother Hugan. 'No more earthquakes. No wild weather. No random electromagnetic pulses firing out into space, crippling spaceships.'

In his peripheral vision, the Doctor could see that Rez had separated from the ever-growing crowd at the entrance. He was slowly crawling around the edge of the massive room.

The lapse in the Doctor's monologue had given Brother Hugan a chance to break free of his spell.

'No!' he cried, raising the knife into the air again.

The Doctor realised that his gambit had failed. Time

for plan D. Or was it E? As usual, he was in danger of running out of code letters for his improvisations.

'Wait,' he cried, dashing forward.

'Keep back,' shouted Brother Hugan warningly.

The Doctor stopped, his hands held out. He flicked the quickest of glances sideways and saw that Rez had reached a statue near to the altar and had begun to climb up it, keeping to the side furthest from the shaman's view. The Doctor just needed to buy him some more time.

'If Laylora needs a sacrifice then give her a proper one,' suggested the Doctor, changing tack.

The shaman waved at the prone figure on the slab of rock before him, enjoying the feel of the mock-Witiku talons as they brushed through Rose's hair.

'I intend to,' he told the Doctor.

'Not her,' said the Doctor dismissively. 'She's no one. Just another human. They're ten a penny.'

Rose, who was stirring back into consciousness, couldn't believe what she was hearing. She half-opened her eyes to try and work out what was going on. Realising that she was lying on the altar stone, it didn't take a great leap of imagination to guess. She didn't dare move as Brother Hugan and his huge knife were too close.

'If you're going to do this properly, sacrifice a real alien,' suggested the Doctor. 'How about one with two hearts? One who's the very last of his kind? Now that's what I call a sacrifice, eh? Am I right or am I right?'

Brother Hugan hesitated, the knife still in mid-air.

'You are offering yourself to die for Laylora?'

'Last of the Time Lords,' said the Doctor, throwing his hands in the air proudly. 'The one and only. A genuine dodo – last specimen of an extinct breed. You want to make a sacrifice to appease the great and bountiful Laylora – better make it a good 'un.'

The Doctor stood waiting for a response. The shaman was clearly mad but not so far gone that he couldn't appreciate an offer like this. Meanwhile, off to one side, Rez had disappeared behind the head of the statue he had climbed. Hopefully he would get around the other side and be in a position to rescue Rose in another few moments. On the altar, Rose was now awake and fully aware of the situation. Her wide eyes met the Doctor's and, to her delight, he winked at her quickly. She prepared herself, cottoning on that he had something in mind.

'Come on, then, old fella. What about it?'

The shaman took a step back, considering. Suddenly a new voice rang out. It was Professor Shulough from the back of the chamber. Kendle had found and untied her during the Doctor's intervention.

'Don't listen to him,' she cried.

The Doctor glared back at her. Not now!

But the professor ignored the look and continued moving forward. 'Don't take him. Take me. It was my spaceship that crashed here. If you want a sacrifice, take me!'

For a moment both the shaman and the Doctor were dumbfounded. Then another new voice was heard.

'No. Not the professor. Take me.' This was Kendle, calling out in a firm voice. Then he too stepped forward and took up a position to one side of the professor.

'No, take me.' This was Hespell, pulling away from Ania Baker, who seemed upset to let him go.

The Doctor smiled. Maybe this was better than his plan. Now, where had Rez got to?

Behind the statue Rez was stuck. He had thought he would be able to sneak round the back of the head of the giant stone Witiku and reach the blind side of Brother Hugan. However, now he realised that the gap between the statue and the wall of the chamber was narrower than he had anticipated.

Taking a deep breath, he tried to squeeze through the narrow gap but only succeeded in getting wedged in place. Now he had no option but to push against the wall with his legs and try to shift the statue enough for him to slip through. It was tough but he was in exactly the right position to gain the necessary leverage.

Slowly, but with increasing speed, the statue was beginning to rock on its base. As yet the movement was not enough to release Rez, but it was only a matter of time. Unfortunately, each forward motion was bringing the statue closer to overbalancing. And from what he could hear, things were coming to a head in front of the altar.

* * *

Brother Hugan looked around him in confusion. Now there was a chorus of offers. From all sides Layloran and human voices called out in turn, offering themselves as sacrifices in place of Rose. For the mentally unstable Brother Hugan, it was utterly overwhelming. He didn't know where to look or what to do.

He clutched one hand to his ear and raised the sacrificial knife high in the air in the other.

'No!' he screamed.

'Now, Rose!' shouted the Doctor at the same moment.

Instantly Rose swung her legs around towards the Doctor and threw herself off of the altar. The Doctor leapt forward to grab her by the arms and pull her to safety. Brother Hugan brought down the knife and cried out in frustration, fury and pain as the blade met the stone altar with a bone-jarring impact at the exact spot where, mere moments ago, Rose had been lying. From above a sudden shadow engulfed him as the statue finally unbalanced and came crashing down. Dust and debris shot into the air as it shattered into hundreds of pieces. The Doctor, still holding on to Rose, rolled clear of the destruction.

For a moment no one dared to breathe. Silence and dust competed to fill the chamber. The Doctor helped Rose to her feet and, without comment, gave her a hug. Finally he spoke to end the deathly quiet.

'Any chance of a nice cup of jinnera, then?'

Smiles and cheerful chatter broke out all around the room.

And then the earthquake hit.

FOURTEEN

Rose grabbed hold of the Doctor, but even braced against each other they could not stay on their feet. Ugly black cracks zigzagged across the floor and in one corner a giant statue fell through into the chamber below. The floor that remained intact reared up at bizarre angles, turning what had been a flat rocky surface into a series of steep-sided islands. Parts of the wall and the ceiling were falling, showering the entire area with yet more dust and rubble.

Somehow the Doctor and Rose managed to cross the broken floor until they reached the relative safety of the corridor. The tunnels, narrow and well constructed, were less vulnerable to the massive earth tremors, which were continuing to shake the world.

'We have to get out,' Rose screamed at the Doctor, who had stopped to look back into the chamber.

'I don't want to leave anyone.'

Although the dust cloud made it difficult to see, it was evident to Rose that most of the people who had been standing near the entrance when the quake struck had escaped into the corridor. She could just make out the shapes of the professor and Kendle a metre or so in front of her through the dust-filled air.

The Doctor was leaning back into the devastated chamber and a moment later it became clear why. The dusty but smiling figure of Rez emerged from the chaos and hurried to join Rose.

'Everyone got out,' he gasped.

'Except Brother Hugan,' added the Doctor grimly. 'Come on!' And he started leading them away.

The aftershocks continued to rumble, causing more rock falls. The entire complex seemed to be shaking itself to pieces. Some loose rocks in the tunnel wall shook free and fell like lethal hailstones. One hit Rose on the side of the head and she stumbled and fell, causing Rez to run into her.

Ahead the Doctor was more concerned with the professor, who had fallen herself and was coughing badly. He helped the older woman to her feet and put an arm round her for support. Kendle came back to assist him.

'I'll get the professor out. She might be concussed,' the Doctor promised him. 'Can you go back and check on Rose and Rez?'

Kendle nodded and hurried back into the dust-filled tunnel. A few metres along he came across the two youngsters, Rez cradling Rose in his arms, and he could see blood on her forehead. Kendle bent and shone a torch on to the cut. To his relief it was just a flesh wound. Rose was already stirring.

'She'll be fine,' he told Rez.

Another aftershock hit, bringing more of the roof down. Kendle bent over the two kids, shielding them with his body. This shower of rocks seemed greater than the last and when the dust settled Kendle was not surprised to find that the tunnel was blocked, cutting them off from the escape route the Doctor and the professor had taken. Not wasting a second, he began to pull at the fallen rocks, but it looked as if this might be an impossible task.

'There's another way,' Rez told him, helping a slightly groggy Rose to her feet.

'Can you show me?' asked Kendle.

'Of course. I know these tunnels backwards,' he said confidently.

'You'd better,' said Kendle grimly, 'because if these shocks get any worse they won't be here much longer.'

Taking his point, Rez started back the way they had just come. Rose and Kendle followed him without further discussion.

Mother Jaelette was waiting for the Doctor as he and the professor emerged into the light. She urged them to get away from the building as quickly as they could, pointing out the damage that it had already suffered. The long, low building that ran alongside the temple had already been flattened and all around them the other buildings that had been standing were now in a state of complete ruin. Here and there massive cracks in the ground itself could be seen. Escaping through the forest was going to be almost as hard as it had been getting out of the underground tunnels.

'Have you seen Rose or Rez?' the Doctor asked urgently.

'Or Major Kendle?' added the professor.

Mother Jaelette shook her head. 'I'm sorry.'

The Doctor looked at the temple, trying to work out if he dare go back inside. The ground buckled under their feet again and, before their horrified eyes, the front half of the building collapsed in on itself. New clouds of dust billowed into the air and the watchers had to stagger away, covering their faces and trying not to breathe in the foul air.

Deep underground the situation beneath the temple was grim. Time and again the three survivors had found their escape route blocked by a fresh rock fall and even Rez was beginning to lose his bearings.

'There must be a way out,' he muttered desperately.

Rose came to a halt. 'Maybe we should just find somewhere that feels safe and sit it out?' she suggested. 'I once hid in a cupboard in 10 Downing Street while the house fell apart around me,' she told them, but just received blank looks in return.

Another wave of aftershocks made them stagger again.

Kendle looked as solemn as ever, even though his face was now coated with a thick layer of dust. 'I don't think we can risk that,' he said firmly. 'We have to get out immediately.'

Rez had pushed on ahead and called back excitedly, 'The staircase!'

Rose and Kendle hurried to join him. They had to scramble over another rock fall to reach it, but Rose was delighted to see that it was the staircase she'd used before. This time there was no hesitation about which direction to take. They started climbing, praying that there would be no further obstacles.

Elsewhere in the rapidly collapsing maze of tunnels a figure stirred and groaned. A fissure had opened up under the altar stone, so instead of being crushed by the falling statue Brother Hugan had been saved.

'Laylora provides,' he muttered, scrambling to his feet.

He pulled off the now ragged Witiku costume and let it fall to the ground. Laylora had saved him again. Truly he was the chosen one.

Nearby a statue of Laylora lay partially buried in rubble. Brother Hugan fell to his knees in front of the cracked face and gave thanks. Kneeling, he brought his head down to touch the ground in front of his goddess.

He felt a burst of energy running through his body and began to shake. It was happening again. The change. He closed his eyes and gave in to the agony and the ecstasy of transformation. He screamed as he felt his limbs stretch and grow. His skin sprouted heavy fur. His bones cracked and re-formed. Once again he was becoming Laylora's champion. She still had need of her Witiku.

Two of the Layloran women were struggling to hold back the Doctor.

'Let me go,' he demanded wildly. 'I have to go back for her.' He shrugged out of his coat, leaving them holding the sleeves, and bolted forwards, but he was immediately knocked off his feet by a violent jolt.

Mother Jaelette shook her head sadly.

'Don't be a fool. Look at it. It would be a suicide to try. There's no way to get in there.'

'There's always a way!' said the Doctor grimly, as Jaelette helped him to his feet.

'I promised her mother that I'd look after her,' he explained in a softer tone.

'Come with me,' Jaelette said gently. 'Let's get clear and wait until the aftershocks stop. Then – when it's safe – we can search for them.'

Still looking over his shoulder at the now almost totally ruined temple complex, the Doctor allowed himself to be led away towards the relative safety of the forest.

So far the staircase was working out. They hadn't come across anything they couldn't scramble over and they had made good progress in getting away from the most dangerous lower levels.

The only problem was that they hadn't found a way out of the stairwell. Rose was fairly certain that they should have passed an exit leading into the main surface-level chamber by now, but they hadn't. There had been one or two places where such an exit might have been, but rock falls had completely filled the archways, making them indistinguishable from the corridors.

Rez was thinking along similar lines. 'The way out at ground level must have been blocked, but we can escape over the roof if necessary,' he told them.

They climbed higher and started to come across narrow window slits, which allowed the light of the twin moons in. They were too narrow to squeeze through but Rose was able to look out and see that they had indeed reached the roof level. They were inside the tower that the Doctor had climbed, which was, almost unbelievably, still standing.

Unfortunately, Rose could now see that there were two routes to the observation post at the top – the path that curved around the outside of the tower and the spiral stone staircase that ran up the middle. The problem was there was no way to get from one to the other except, presumably, at the very top. Which meant that with every step the three humans were getting higher and higher above the roof of the temple.

Rose looked out of another slit of a window and

surveyed the state of the temple below. It was not looking great. A huge part of the front of the building had already collapsed and she feared the rest would go the same way at any moment. Then she heard something that was even more frightening. Something clambering up the staircase after her. Something big and angry. A moment later they all heard the familiar roar. A Witiku. They had no choice but to continue their ascent.

The Doctor looked back from the forest at the scene of destruction. The earthquake had been a major one and the aftershocks continued to come every couple of minutes. Each one was accompanied by the sound of further damage to the temple site. The cellars and underground passages were falling in on themselves and much of the area now resembled a quarry.

He was using tiny electronic night-vision binoculars to scan the area of the main temple for any sign of Rose. There was little to show now that the temple itself had until recently been in a better condition than the other buildings surrounding it. Now there was a gaping hole to the front of the complex that extended for about fifty metres. By the Doctor's reckoning, most of the subterranean areas must have been destroyed and it was only a matter of time before what was left on the surface went the same way. Where was Rose?

He moved his view upwards, noting that the central

observation tower was still intact. It had taken on a slight tilt, reminiscent of the Leaning Tower of Pisa, but that was the current extent of the damage. He thought he saw a movement and switched the device to maximum magnification. This was enough for the whole of one of the window slits to fill his screen and now he could make out figures. Rose, thank goodness, followed by Rez and then the sturdy figure of Kendle. All three were safe – at least for the moment. But then he realised that there was a fourth shape moving, lower down the tower. He refocused his viewer and gasped in surprise. A Witiku! Had they missed one? Whatever the explanation, the creature was hot on the heels of Rose and her friends. The Doctor had to do something and, whatever it was, he had to do it fast.

Nearby the professor and her two remaining crew members were recovering from their ordeal. The Doctor hurried over to them, pulling out a handful of trisilicate crystals from his pockets.

'Do you think this is enough trisilicate to get your ship in the air?' he asked.

Rose couldn't believe that she was still running – and up steps now. It was clear to all of them that they remained in terrible danger. Kendle had fired a few warning shots from his laser blaster back down the staircase, but the curvature of the stairs made it impossible to get a clear shot. It bought Rose and Rez some time to put some distance between them and the

Witiku, however, so Kendle kept dropping back and firing, before turning and sprinting up the steps behind them. They'd been through this routine twice now and it was taking its toll on all of them.

'I'm getting too old for this,' Kendle gasped, as he caught up with the two youngsters again.

'How old are you?' asked Rose, her curiosity getting the better of her sense of politeness.

'Sixty-eight a week next Tuesday,' he told her. 'And not ready to cash in my chips yet.'

'Sixty-eight?' she repeated. 'That's nothing. The Doctor's 900 and something,' she told him, 'and look at him – he's still going strong.' She grinned at the bemused looks on their faces.

But, having allowed themselves a moment's pause, they began climbing again. A few seconds later the staircase opened out into a wider space, covered with a pyramid-shaped roof it was the observation deck. Across the way, Rose could see the exit that led to the external staircase.

She hurried over to take a look. It seemed a long way down. Kendle was checking out the possibilities of the room for defence.

'We should try and hold this position,' he announced.

'What?' Rose didn't understand. 'Shouldn't we start going down now?'

Kendle shook his head. 'We'd be too vulnerable. It's totally exposed. Another aftershock and we could go flying. And our hairy friend below could just leap down on top of us. We'd be best holding here and trying to neutralise the enemy combatant.'

'What do you mean "neutralise"?' demanded Rez, unfamiliar with the term.

Rose understood. It was military speak. 'You mean kill him, don't you?'

Kendle nodded and checked his weapon.

'And then what?' asked Rez.

Kendle shrugged. 'If I'm successful we can descend in relative safety. If I'm not, it'll be academic.'

Kendle moved to take up position at the head of the stairwell. The roar of the lone Witiku was close now. A moment later the hairy beast swung into sight. Kendle fired his weapon, shooting a massive hole in the wall and forcing it back. The creature roared furiously and then went quiet. Rez and Rose looked at each other. What next? Rose sat down heavily and put her head in her hands. Wherever he was, she really needed the Doctor now.

The Doctor was concentrating hard, taking in the complex bank of controls in front of him. He was sitting in the pilot's chair on board the bridge of the *Humphrey Bogart*. Alongside him, Ania Baker and Jonn Hespell had worried expressions on their young faces. It had taken them three years at the academy to get the most basic piloting qualification and now the Doctor was proposing to fly the ship, as an aircraft, with barely a read-through of the manual.

'Are you sure you don't want me to pilot her?' asked Hespell.

'Positive. You've only trained to fly in deep space, haven't you?' the Doctor replied.

Hespell shrugged. 'Well, yes, but at least I'm familiar with the control systems.'

The Doctor shot him a confident look. 'Up, down, forward, back. What else is there to know?'

Baker reached across to grab Hespell's hand and gave him a sympathetic look. He smiled back, pleased that she was there with him.

'Right, then,' announced the Doctor, clapping his hands. 'Let's get started. Fire retros.'

'Retros in three, two, one. Retros fired,' Baker announced calmly.

'Release gravity locks.'

'Releasing.'

For a moment everything seemed to be frozen. And then the Doctor eased the control joystick forward slightly and the ship began to rise.

Rose realised that things had gone quiet. She raised her head and looked back down the stairs. Kendle was still concentrating on the stairwell. Despite the lack of pursuit sounds, he remained suspicious.

'Perhaps he's given up and gone away?' Rose said quietly.

Kendle shook his head. 'I doubt it.'

Then, from some way below, they heard crashing and banging. Rocks and debris were falling from the exterior of the tower.

'What's it trying to do? Bring the tower down?' Rez asked.

'I don't like the sound of that,' commented Kendle, taking a cautious step down the staircase. 'Whatever it is, I think I should go and… well, try to persuade him to stop.' He took another two or three steps and began to disappear around the stairwell.

'Be careful,' called out Rose.

'And you,' he shouted back.

Rose looked across at Rez, who was leaning on the wall and staring out over his world.

'Just you and me, then,' she said, getting to her feet and joining him.

It was a magnificent sight. It must be nearly dawn – the sky was beginning to lighten. Just like the Doctor had told her, Rose could see for miles in every direction. And, even after the earthquake, it was beautiful. Suddenly she became aware of something in her peripheral vision. She looked down and saw to her horror that the Witiku was on the external staircase. It must have knocked a hole through the wall to get out there and was now rapidly closing in on their position from outside.

Rose pulled Rez away from the edge as it reached a position just a metre or so from the base of the observation platform. But now a new noise was filling the air and a dark shadow was blocking out the rising sun. Rose protected her face with an arm and squinted up. It was the *Humphrey Bogart*! The Doctor had come back for them!

The battered ship was approaching in hover mode. Rose could see that the airlock was open and, inside, she could make out the professor and Hespell. Slowly the ship edged sideways towards them.

'Our ride's here,' Rose called down to Kendle.

'And so's our other friend,' added Rez, in a tone of panic.

Rose turned and saw that the Witiku was standing in the gap that allowed access to the external staircase. She recognised the fancy necklace hanging around its neck.

'It's Brother Hugan,' she gasped, as the creature leapt forward, swinging its arms down towards them, determined not to let them get away again.

Rose and Rez dived to either side as the creature's talons scraped into the stone floor, sending sparks flying. They scrambled to their feet as it turned for a second attack.

The spaceship was now a metre or two away from the observation platform. It was a spectacular display of precision flying. One mistake now and the Doctor would send the ship into the tower, making a bad situation worse rather than better.

From inside the airlock the professor called out to them. 'Jump!'

Rose swallowed hard. Was she serious? The professor was screaming into the intercom now. 'Closer!' she ordered whoever was piloting the ship. Rose guessed it had to be the Doctor.

Rez took a look at the leap and grinned. 'Now or never,' he shouted to Rose, and started to run. He took off like a long-jumper and seemed to hang in the air for eternity. And then – clang! – he was landing on the metal floor of the airlock and Professor Shulough was hauling him in. 'Your turn, Rose!' he called back across the gaping chasm.

Rose crossed her fingers and ran. She ducked past the creature and jumped into space. A moment later she felt the professor and Hespell grab hold of her and pull her to safety. She turned to look back across at the platform.

The transformed Brother Hugan was snapping at her heels. And then the creature lurched and fell to its knees. Behind it stood Kendle, weapon in hand. Unbelievably, the Witiku just rolled over and got back on his feet.

Rose and the others could only look on in mute horror as the old soldier and the transformed Layloran confronted each other. Kendle raised his weapon and fired again, but the Witiku just kept coming. Kendle fired repeatedly, but the Witiku only swiped impatiently at the blaster with a sweep of one of his powerful arms.

'I can't hold this position much longer.' It was the

Doctor's voice cackling out of the intercom speaker. 'There was only time to part-charge the engines.'

The Doctor's problems were becoming evident as the ship began to rock violently.

'Just one more minute,' urged the professor desperately.

'Get clear,' shouted Kendle, and jumped forward, surprising the Witiku with a frontal attack. He swung both fists up and his double punch connected with the creature's jaw.

As the ship bobbed up and down, it was hard for Rose to see exactly what was happening but the next thing she saw haunted her for a long time. The two combatants, the ex-marine and the bestial Witiku, staggered to the edge of the platform and then fell together, still locked in combat. The fall seemed to happen in slow motion, the two figures crashing again and again into the widening tower, bouncing off like rag dolls before finally coming to rest on the shattered roof of the temple.

Without a word the professor hit the control to close the outer doors and the ship moved away to find a safe place to land.

FIFTEEN

Rose stood at the entrance to the tent and looked out at the storm. Although it was daylight, the sky was dark with clouds and the rain was coming down in sheets. A heavy rumble of thunder was followed by a sharp crack of lightning, splitting the deep purple of the sky. The storm had been raging for hours now and showed no signs of abating.

'So much for paradise,' she commented, turning back to where the Doctor was sitting with Mother Jaelette and some of the village elders.

'As soon as the storm breaks the *Humphrey Bogart* will take off,' promised the Doctor confidently. 'But they are not going to risk their shields in the kind of lightning out there right now,' he added.

'Is that what made them crash in the first place?' Rose wondered.

'Hespell said it was some kind of electromagnetic pulse. My bet is that's another way the planet reacts to anything alien. The same thing that damaged Guillan's ship fifty years ago.' The Doctor shook his head in disbelief. 'It really is the most hyper-allergic place I've ever seen. Anyway, once the ship takes off things will get back to normal.'

'What about us?' Rose asked.

The Doctor grinned. 'Well, obviously we have to get going too. I'm sure Laylora is as allergic to us as she is to the crew of the *Humphrey Bogart*.'

'That still leaves me, though, doesn't it?'

Rose had forgotten Rez, who was sitting with Kaylen at the rear of the tent. In his Layloran clothes, Rez looked at first glance to be no different from any of the other natives, but of course he was no more a native than Rose was.

'It's all my fault, isn't it? The bad weather, the earth tremors... Everything started when I arrived, didn't it?' Rose could see that Rez already knew the answer to his question and was resigned to it.

The Doctor knew it too. 'I think so. The older you got, the worse the allergic reaction. The arrival of the *Humphrey Bogart* was the straw that broke the camel's back.'

'I don't know what to do. All I've ever known is life on Laylora.' Rez sounded genuinely heartbroken.

'I'm sure we can take you somewhere you'll be happy, can't we?' Rose looked to the Doctor for approval, but he was on his feet and at the tent flap.

'Looks like the rain's stopping,' he muttered,

avoiding the question. 'Let's go and see the *Humphrey Bogart* off.'

Rose turned and shrugged apologetically at the others before following him.

The Doctor was right, as usual. The rain quickly became drizzle, then stopped altogether and the more usual sunshine began to appear. By the time the Doctor and Rose had reached the spaceship, the weather was back to the summer holiday paradise that they had first landed in. The heat of the sun quickly evaporated the dampness left from the last of the rain.

At the *Humphrey Bogart* they were greeted by Hespell and Baker, who told them that the ship was ready to launch and that the professor was completing the final checks. The Doctor said that he needed a word with her and disappeared, leaving Rose with the two young crew members.

Hespell and Baker were standing together, not holding hands or touching but clearly a couple.

'I hear congratulations are in order,' Rose said with a smile. Both Hespell and Baker blushed. 'Hey, it's OK. Nothing wrong with a little office romance,' she told them.

The pair exchanged a look. 'It's not really what we expected to find on this mission,' confessed Hespell.

'Isn't that the best kind of discovery?' asked Rose. 'You came looking for paradise and ended up finding each other. That's a result, isn't it?'

Baker grinned and slipped an arm around her new boyfriend. 'Yes, I think it is.'

The bridge was deserted but the Doctor guessed where the professor would be and headed for her quarters. As expected, Professor Shulough was looking through her paradise files, slowly putting all her material back in boxes. The Doctor knocked politely on the open door and stepped into the room.

'I'm sorry about your uncle,' he said.

The professor looked up and he could see that she had been crying.

'Thank you. He died a soldier's death, protecting others. It's what he would have wanted.'

For a long moment there was silence as the Doctor watched her putting away the artefacts and mementoes that had ruled her life for so long.

'You know that this place has to be taken off the maps again, don't you?'

The professor nodded sadly. 'Shame, isn't it?'

'Better paradise lost than paradise never seen,' suggested the Doctor kindly.

She laughed. 'I suppose that's one way of looking at it.' She was silent for a moment, then said more thoughtfully, 'You were right the other day, you know, when you said we were being attacked by environmentalists. We arrive somewhere wonderful and instantly destroy it, just by being there. Humans should be the social outcasts of the cosmos.'

The Doctor shook his head. 'You're being too hard on your race. Humans are incredible. Go anywhere in the known universe and you'll find their traces. You've achieved so much, gone so far. From one little planet. I think it's remarkable!'

'But everywhere we go, don't we ultimately bring destruction?'

The Doctor couldn't go along with that conclusion. 'No, that's just not true. You make mistakes, sure, but you never give up. That's what I love about the human race. I wouldn't have hung around with you lot for this long if I didn't believe in "humanity".'

The professor placed Guillan's journal back in the box on top of her other papers and put the lid on. When she rose she was smiling.

'Thanks,' she said with genuine warmth. 'That makes me feel better.'

'There was one more thing,' the Doctor added, and then hesitated before continuing.

'You're going to ask me about the boy, aren't you?' She looked quizzically at the Doctor.

'He's got no one.'

'He has now,' the professor assured him. 'I'm probably too old to be much of a mother. That was never going to be my story. But I can be a guardian and a guide.'

'He'll need that,' the Doctor said, smiling.

The professor sat down and put her face in her hands. Something about her seemed to have changed since her adventures in the temple.

'It hurt me so much, when my parents died,' she began to explain in a quiet voice. 'I promised myself I'd never feel like that again.' She looked up at the Doctor with tears in her eyes. 'I thought if I didn't allow myself to get close to anyone, I'd be protected.'

The Doctor nodded sympathetically.

'But I was wrong, wasn't I?'

'Life hurts,' agreed the Doctor. 'Things change, people come and go, nothing lasts. But if you don't engage with people, if you don't allow yourself to care...' He stopped and let the thought hang in the air for a moment. 'Well, if you do that, then you're not really alive, are you?'

The professor looked into the Doctor's eyes and realised that all the pain she felt when her parents died was nothing in comparison to the heartache this alien had known. She looked away, not wanting to intrude.

'I'll see what I can do,' she said after a long silence. 'About the boy.'

The Doctor headed for the door. 'Thank you,' he whispered, and then he was gone.

Rose found Rez sitting at the edge of the clearing made by the *Humphrey Bogart* when it first landed. The Doctor had returned the ship to precisely the same spot it had originally occupied, to minimise the impact on the sensitive planet. Rez was looking at it now, a curious expression on his face.

Rose sat down beside him on the soft grass. 'Penny for them,' she asked.

He frowned, not understanding.

'It's an expression,' she explained. 'It means what are you thinking?'

He nodded his head in the direction of the spaceship.

'What's it like out there?' he asked her.

Rose hesitated. How could she possibly answer that? The Doctor had explained to her that he thought it best if Rez went with the crew of the *Humphrey Bogart* and she realised that he was probably right. Poor Rez. No wonder he was looking scared. What a challenge!

'You'll love it,' she said finally, after long consideration. 'It's an adventure.'

Rez smiled. 'Have you been travelling for a long time?'

'It's hard to say,' she confessed, 'but however long it's been, it's not been long enough. There's so much out there to discover. Some of it is dangerous and some of it is ugly, but it's never dull.'

She reached out and patted his hand.

'You can trust me on this.' And she smiled to herself, thinking of her own father. 'You never know, you may have family out there, waiting to meet you.'

When the time came for the final round of goodbyes it seemed to take for ever. Watching it all, Rose realised why the Doctor preferred to slip away normally rather than get caught up in protracted farewells. On this occasion, however, he had declared that they had a duty to stay and see things through to the bitter end.

Hespell and Baker had disappeared into the spaceship to take their places, leaving the professor waiting for Rez. He was doing an endless round of hugs with various Laylorans, finally coming to his adopted mother and sister. Both Jaelette and Kaylen had tears in their eyes, but, despite a trembling lip, Rez was managing to hold it together. Jaelette and Kaylen gripped Rez tight and squeezed hard, knowing that they were unlikely ever to see him again.

Finally Rez prised himself loose and joined Professor Shulough, who led him into the airlock. As the doors closed, Rez looked back one last time at his paradise home and then turned away.

The Doctor and Rose ushered Jaelette, Kaylen and the other Laylorans away from the ship as Hespell ignited the manoeuvring thrusters and the huge metal ship slowly lifted off the ground.

Surprisingly graceful, it gained height and then speed as it cleared the trees and reached the open sky. Then, shifting to antigravity engines, it accelerated and quickly headed off into space. Within a minute there was nothing to see but a dot in the sky and a moment later even that had disappeared completely.

The Doctor and Rose walked back to the TARDIS in silence, deep in their own thoughts. Rose took the opportunity to take one last look at the wonderful planet and her heart went out to poor Rez, who had been forced to leave this paradise.

'Will he be all right?' she wondered out loud.

'I think so,' the Doctor answered after a moment or two. 'Humans are very adaptable.'

'But this is all he's ever known.'

'Until now.' The Doctor smiled. 'Anyway, it's the only way this place can get back to its normal state.'

'A paradise planet that no human can ever visit. That's a bit sad, isn't it?'

The Doctor shrugged, searching in his pocket for the TARDIS key.

'You know that feeling on a winter's day, when it's snowed in the night and you come downstairs and everything is different. There's a blanket of white and it's all perfect, untouched?'

'Yeah,' Rose said, 'and you want to go out in it but at the same time you don't, 'cause then it'll get mushy and covered in footprints and… spoilt.'

The Doctor nodded. 'It's the same thing here. Nothing lasts for ever, not even the Paradise Planet. But it can last for a bit longer yet.'

He opened the door and stepped through into the impossibly cavernous console room of his own ship. Rose hesitated for a moment in the doorway, looking back at the beach.

'Oh, well,' she said, following the Doctor and closing the TARDIS door behind her, 'there's always Clacton, I suppose. Not much call for a bikini there, though.'

The Doctor was already at the controls, setting switches and preparing to dematerialise.

'I think we can do a bit better than that,' he said, grinning. He pulled at a lever and set the central column in motion. 'Let's go and explore!'

Between the beautiful beach and the fantastic forest a wind whipped up out of nowhere and, with a wild trumpeting sound, the blue police box exterior of the TARDIS gently faded from view.

Elsewhere, the SS *Humphrey Bogart*, battered and ugly, punched a hole into hyperspace and disappeared from view.

'Here,' said the professor, setting a mug of a hot liquid in front of the young man who was now dressed in a spare uniform.

Rez took the mug and sniffed suspiciously.

The professor smiled, taking years off her age. 'I made sure I took some jinnen with us. Can't expect you to get used to tea overnight, can we?'

Rez took a grateful sip. It was a little on the weak side but he kept quiet about it, not wanting to upset his new guardian.

He studied the woman who had promised to look after him in this strange new life. She seemed more relaxed now, younger, even though she had been forced to abandon her long-sought paradise. She was looking through the scant possessions that he had brought on board with him and held up the strange cube that had been packed into his escape pod.

'Do you know what this is?' she asked him.

Rez shook his head. He'd spent hours looking at it over the years but its meaning had always eluded him. It was just a plain plastic cube as far as he knew.

'It's a memory cube,' she told him, and started running her fingers over each of the surfaces, looking around for something.

'Ah!' she exclaimed, as she found the hidden switches that she knew had to be there.

The cube lit up as it burst into life. A hologram field sprang into view above one of the sides and the cube started to run a program. The hologram showed two humans, a handsome but slightly worried-looking man and a beautiful young woman with long blonde hair.

They began to talk to the baby son they were about to place in an escape pod. Rez watched and listened, tears rolling down his face. His parents were long dead, but here at last they were able to speak to him.

Petra Shulough moved across the room to sit next to him and placed an arm around his shoulders.

'Now we can find out who you are and where you came from,' she whispered to him gently.

She realised that she had been given a new and much more valuable quest to follow, and this time she would not be alone.

Acknowledgements

I am indebted to a number of people who have helped me in producing this novel and would like to take this opportunity to thank them all.

First, everyone at BBC Worldwide, especially Stuart Cooper, Kate Walsh, my patient and talented copy-editor, Lesley Levene, and Justin Richards, the creative director of these books, who gave me the chance to be here.

I'd also like to thank my fellow writers in this line, Stephen Cole, Steve Lyons, Jac Rayner, Gareth Roberts, Mike Tucker and Justin Richards (again), for inspiration and for setting the standard so high!

I must also thank my very patient wife, Kerry – always my first editor – and my children, Cefn and Kassia, who have all been very understanding during this book's accelerated production process.

Finally, I want to thank everyone at BBC Wales and in the BBC Drama Department who have worked so hard to produce the wonderful revival of *Doctor Who* on television. In particular I must thank Helen Raynor, my point of contact in the *Doctor Who* Script Department, and, of course, the main man, Russell T Davies, whom I want to thank particularly for the opportunity to be (a small) part of this splendid new era of *Doctor Who*. Thank you all.

About the Author

Colin Brake has stopped counting birthdays and given up measuring his height! As a writer and script editor he has been involved in the television business for twenty years. He has worked on shows as diverse as *EastEnders*, *Trainer* and *Bugs* and written scripts for many programmes, including over thirty episodes of the BBC daytime soap *Doctors*.

Having been thwarted in his ambition to become the next script editor of *Doctor Who* back in 1989, when the BBC cancelled the programme, he is rather amazed to find that he has now written Doctor Who audio plays, short stories and novels.

He lives in Leicester with his wife, Kerry, their two children, Cefn and Kassia, and two Cornish Rex cats who love to walk all over his keyboard and thus get the blame for all typos (the cats, that is, not the children – although they too have their moments!).

DOCTOR·WHO

Aliens and Enemies

By Justin Richards

ISBN-10 0 563 48632 5

ISBN-13 978 0 563 48646 6

UK £7.99 US $12.99/$15.99 CDN

The Cybermen are back to terrorise time and space – but luckily the new Doctor, played by David Tennant, and Rose are back to stop them.

Picking up where Monsters and Villains left off, this fully illustrated guide documents the return of these metal menaces, as well as the Sycorax and other foes from the new series, plus first series terrors like the Gelth and the Reapers.

More classic baddies such as the dreaded Zarbi, Sutekh and the Robots of Death also make a welcome appearance.

The Nightmare of Black Island

By Mike Tucker

ISBN-10 0 563 48650 3
ISBN-13 978 0 563 48650 3
UK £6.99 US $11.99/$14.99 CDN

On a lonely stretch of Welsh coastline a fisherman is killed by a hideous creature from beneath the waves. When the Doctor and Rose arrive, they discover a village where the children are plagued by nightmares, and the nights are ruled by monsters. The villagers suspect that ailing industrialist Nathanial Morton is to blame, but the Doctor has suspicions of his own.

Who are the ancient figures that sleep in the old priory? And what is the light that glows in the disused lighthouse on Black Island?

As the children's nightmares get worse, the Doctor and Rose discover an alien plot to resurrect an ancient evil…

The Art of Destruction

By Stephen Cole

ISBN-10 0 563 48651 1

ISBN-13 978 0 563 48651 0

UK £6.99 US $11.99/$14.99 CDN

The TARDIS lands in 22nd-century Africa in the shadow of a dormant volcano. Agri-teams are growing new foodstuffs in the baking soil to help feed the world's starving millions – but the Doctor and Rose have detected an alien signal somewhere close by.

When a nightmare force starts surging along the dark volcanic tunnels, the Doctor realises an ancient trap has been sprung. But who was it meant for? And what is the secret of the eerie statues that stand at the heart of the volcano?

Dragged into a centuries-old conflict, Rose and the Doctor have to fight for their lives as alien hands practice the arts of destruction all around them.